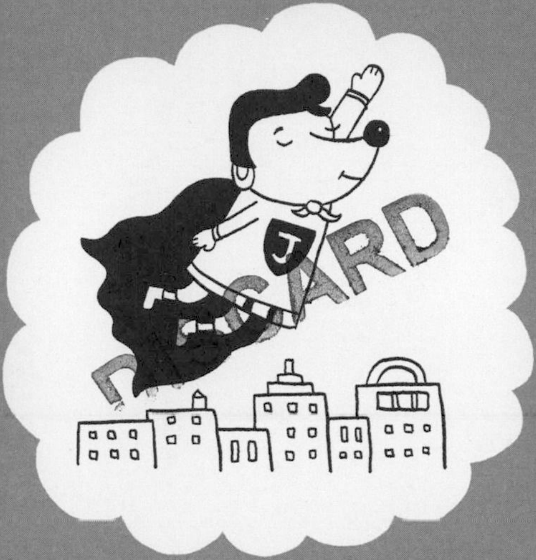

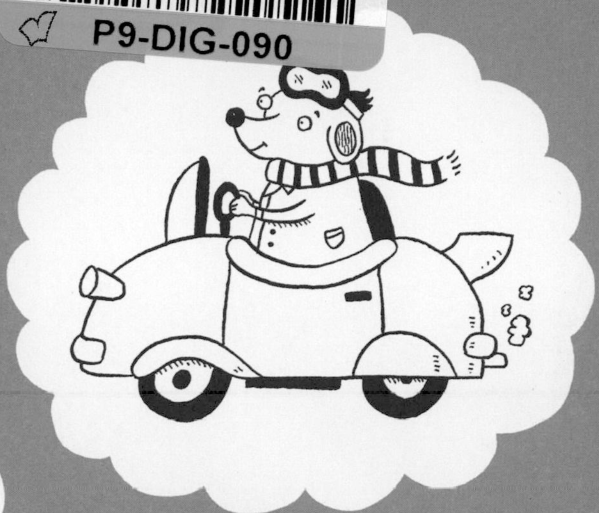

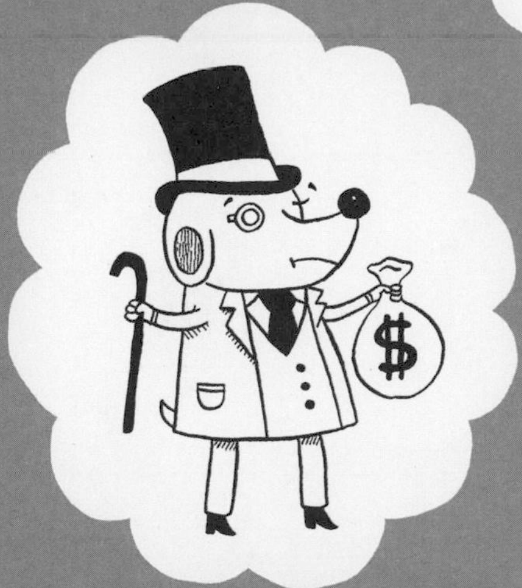
$

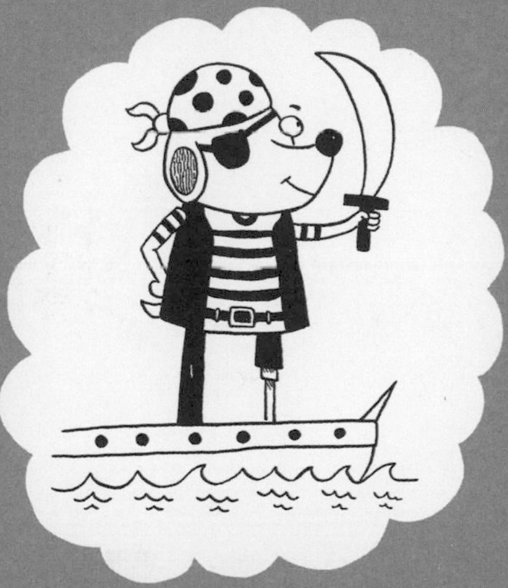

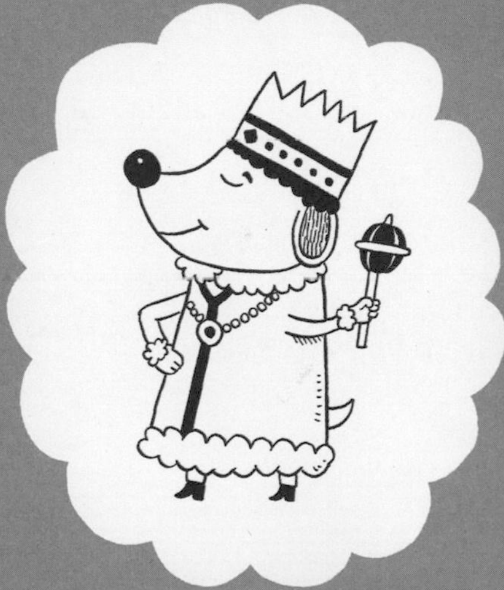

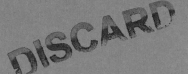

Copyright ©2011 Mike Herrod

Balloon Toons™ is a registered

trademark of Harriet Ziefert, Inc.

All rights reserved/CIP data is available.

Published in the United States 2011 by

Blue Apple Books

515 Valley Street, Maplewood, NJ 07040

www.blueapplebooks.com

First Edition 03/11
Printed in China
ISBN: 978-1-60905-065-8

2 4 6 8 10 9 7 5 3 1

BALLOON TOONS™

Mike Herrod's

Doggie Dreams

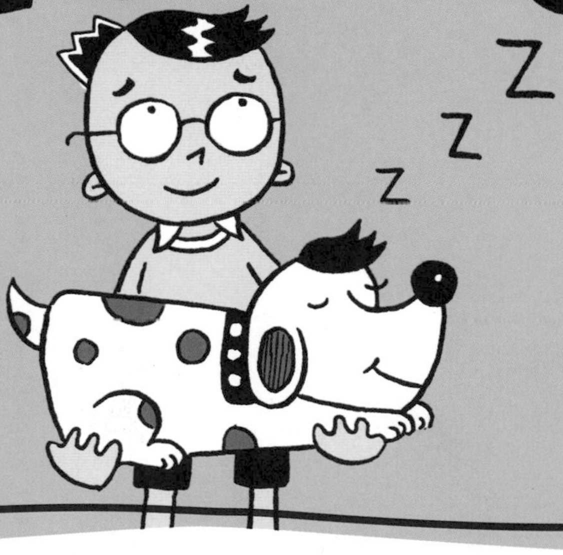

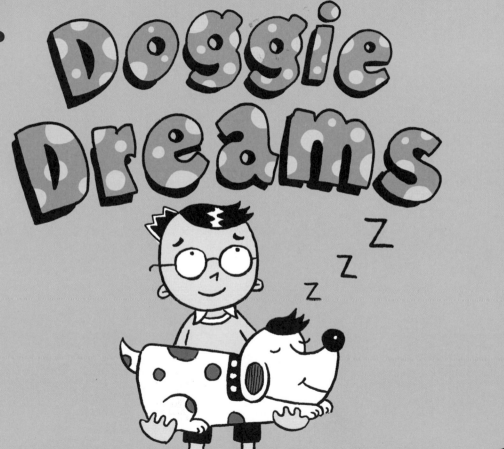

BLUE APPLE BOOKS

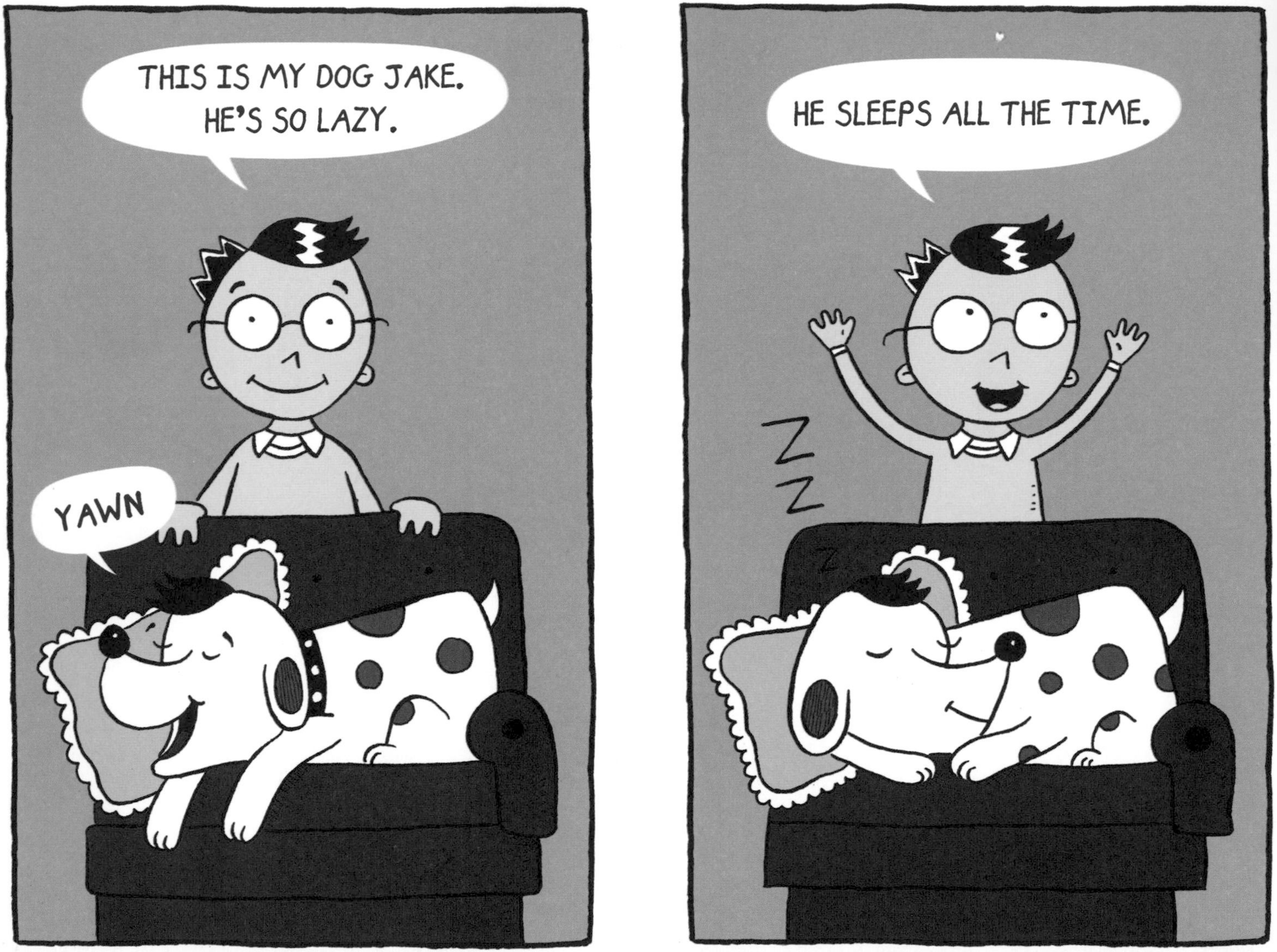
THIS IS MY DOG JAKE.
HE'S SO LAZY.
YAWN
HE SLEEPS ALL THE TIME.
Z Z
Z

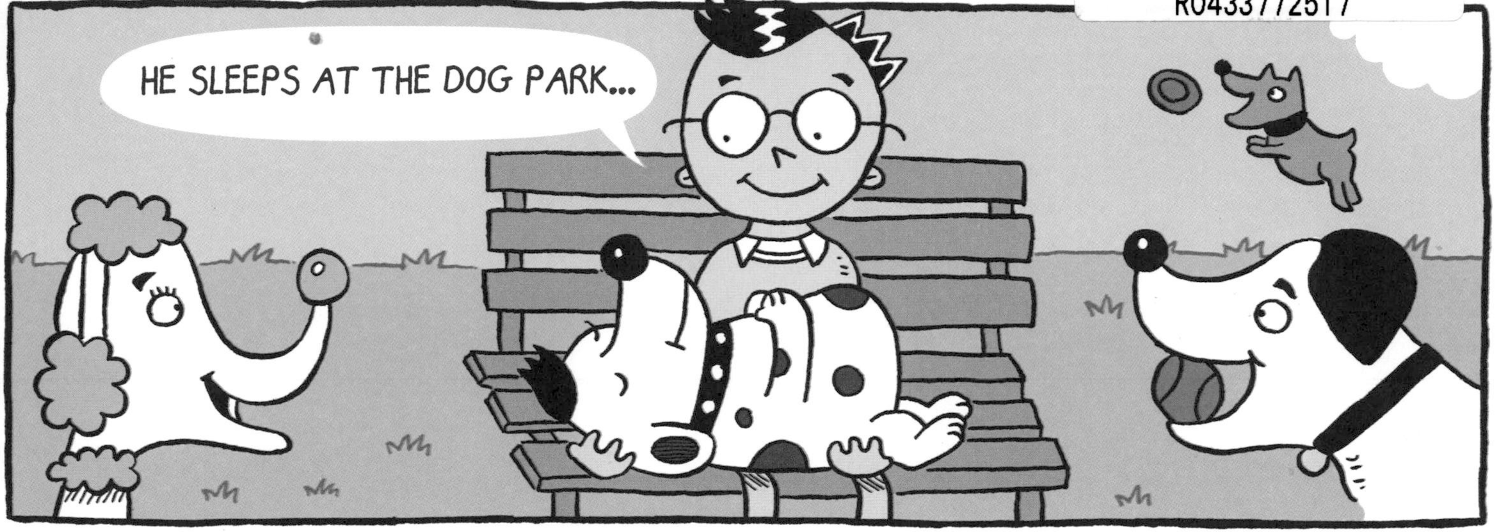
HE SLEEPS AT THE DOG PARK...

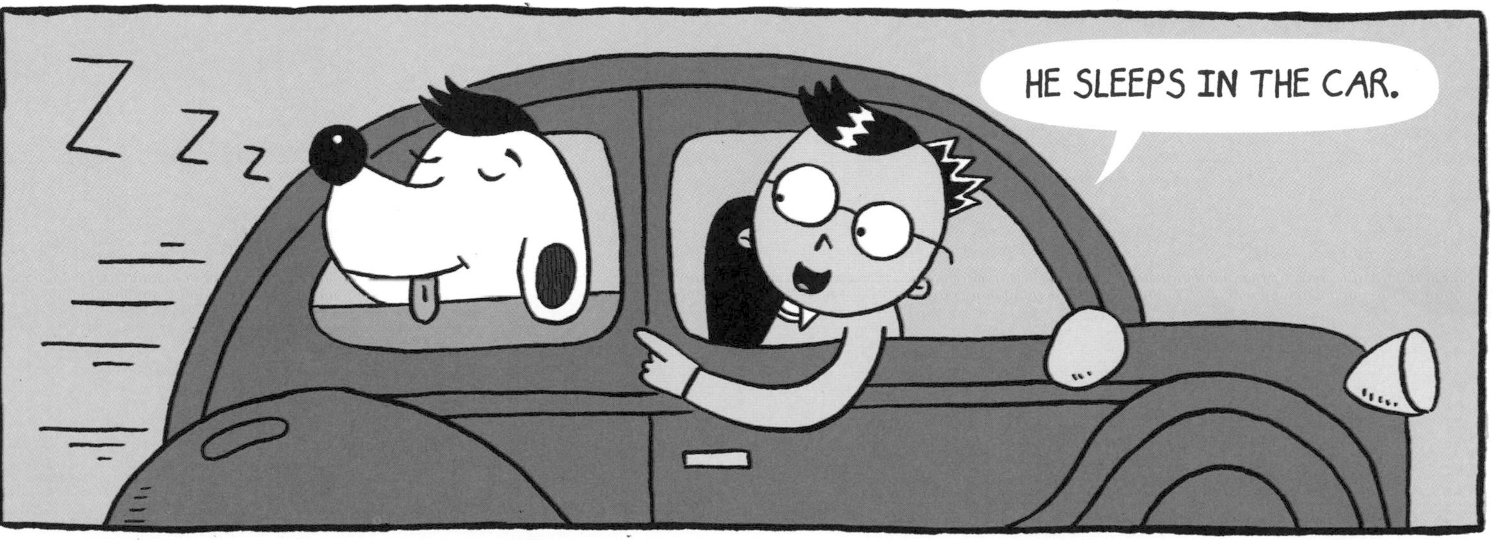
Z Z z
HE SLEEPS IN THE CAR.

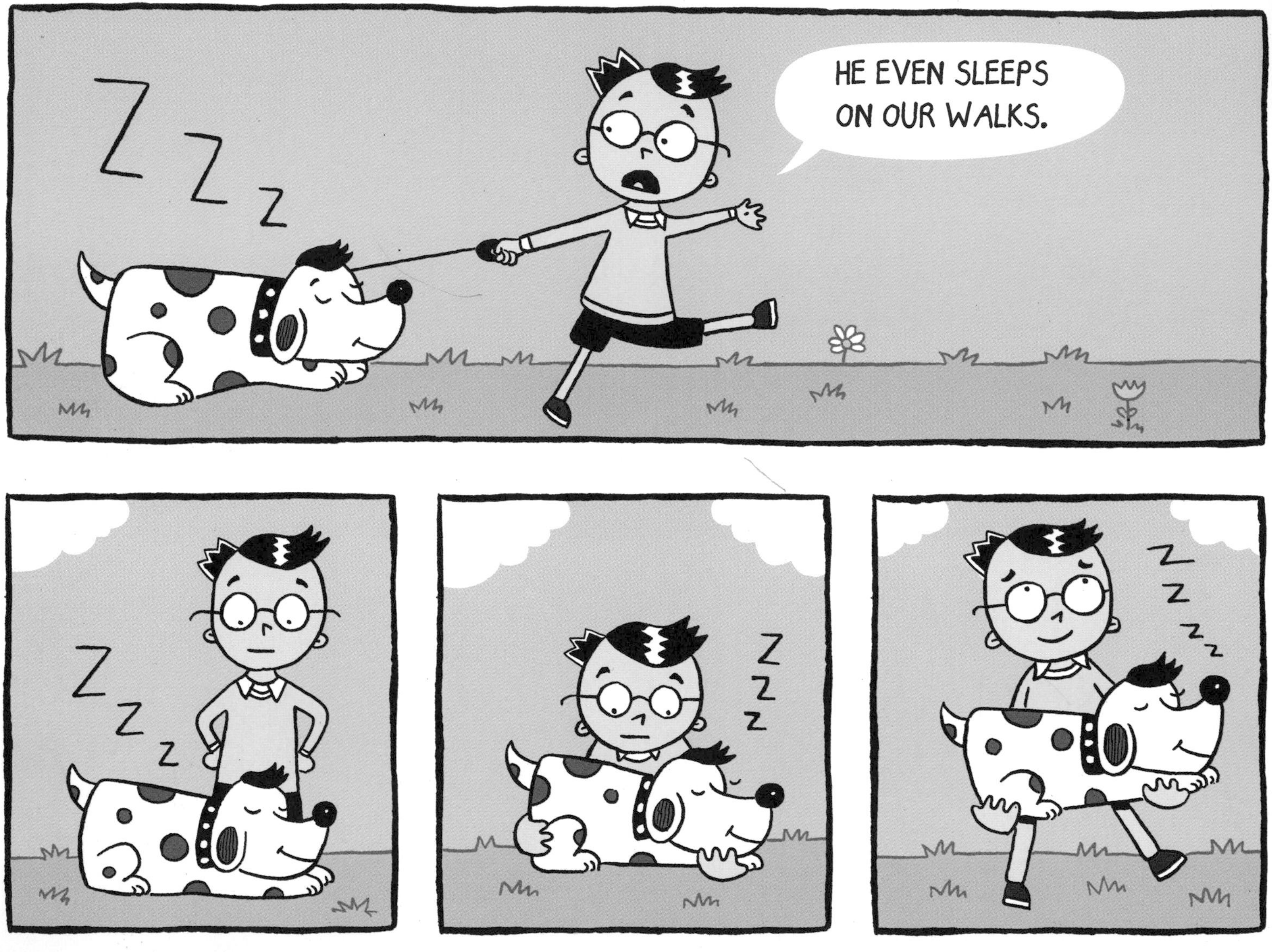
Z Z Z
HE EVEN SLEEPS ON OUR WALKS.
Z Z Z
Z Z Z
Z Z Z Z

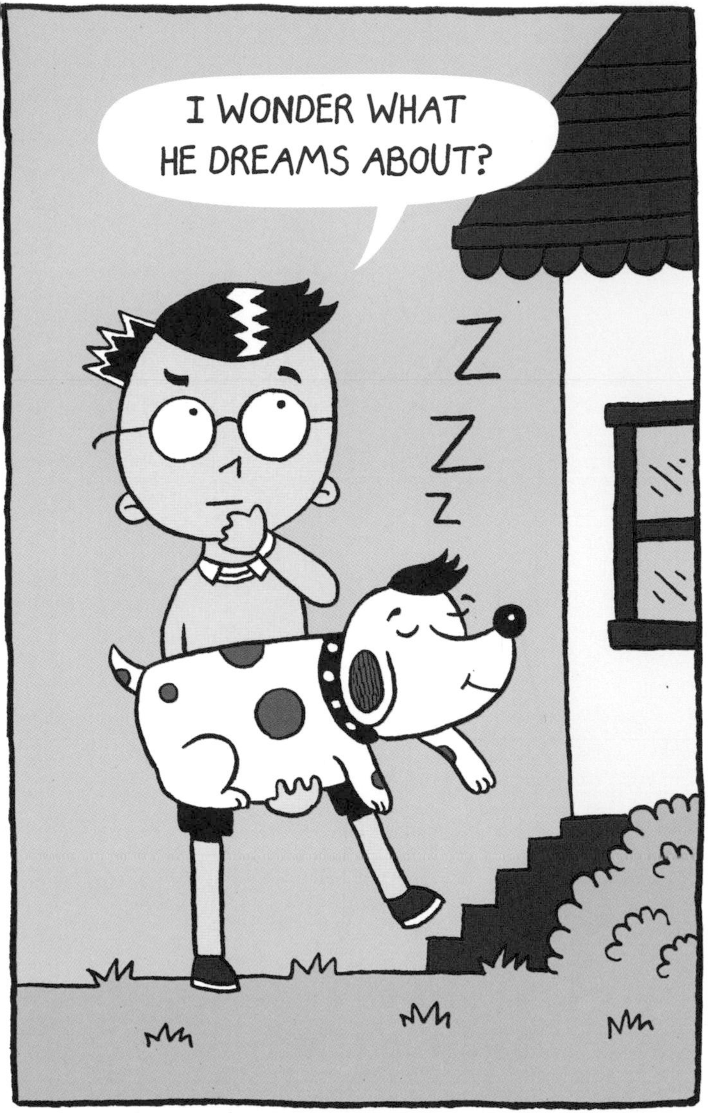
I WONDER WHAT HE DREAMS ABOUT?
Z Z Z

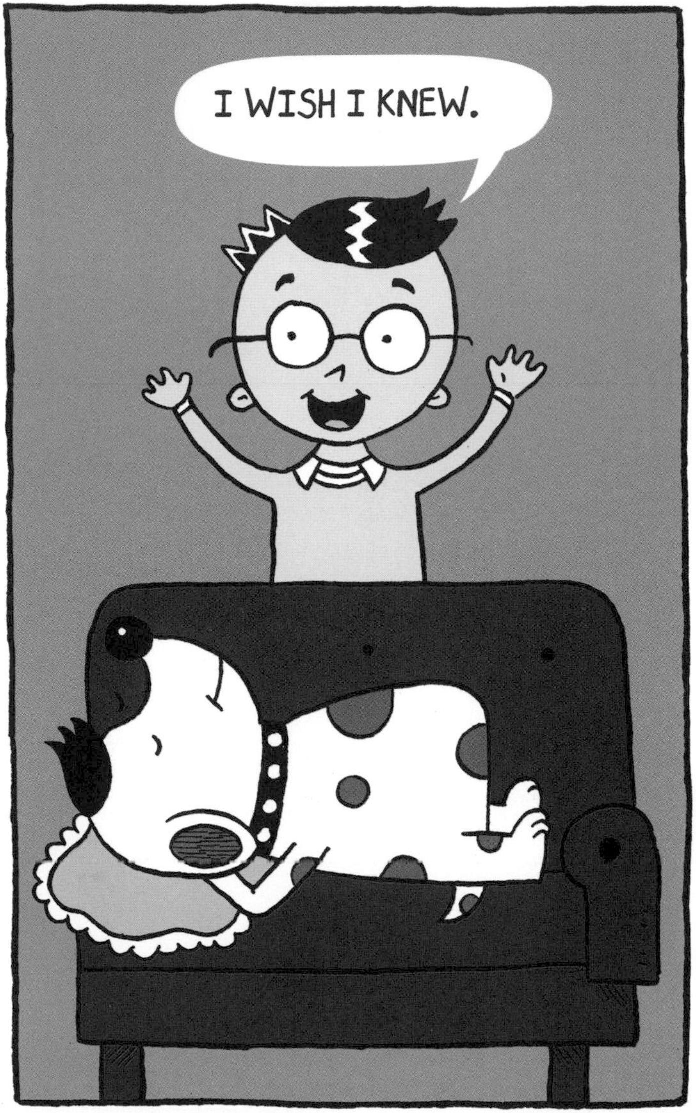
I WISH I KNEW.

DREAM #1: Bone Appétit!

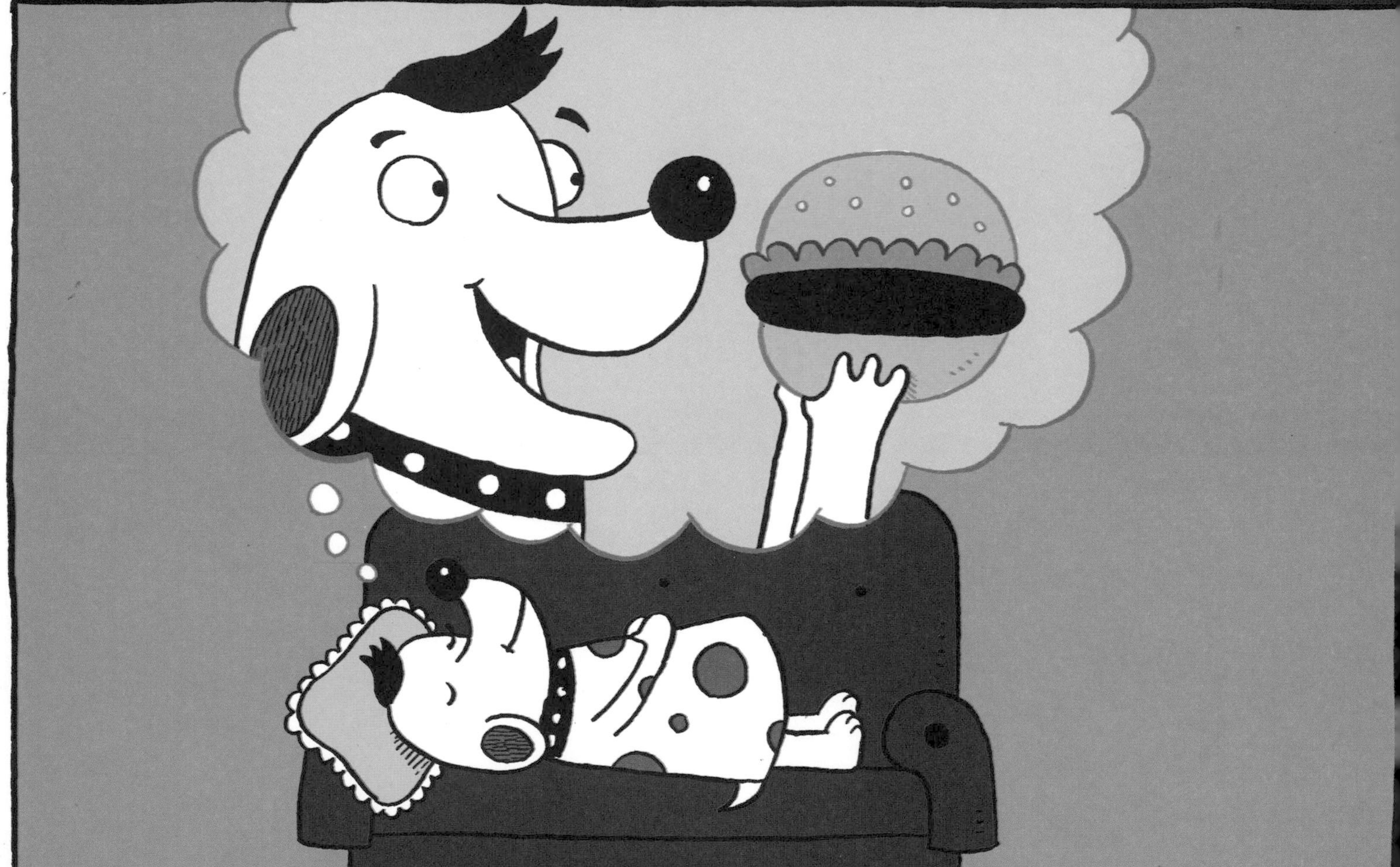

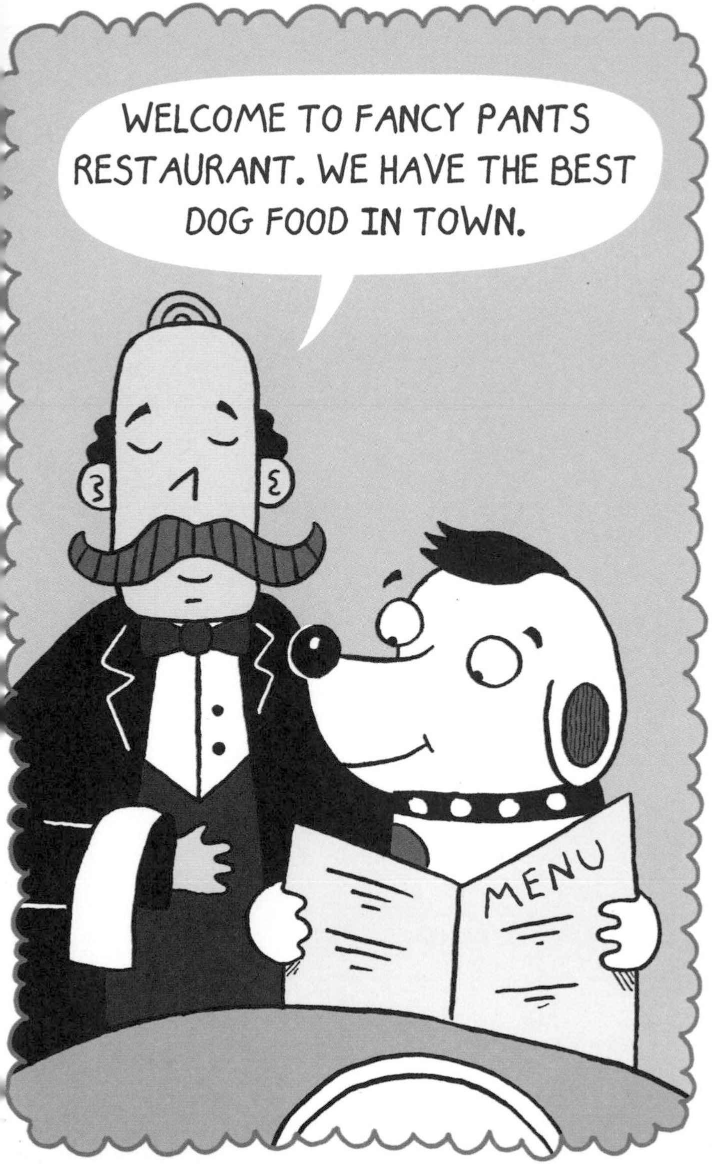
WELCOME TO FANCY PANTS RESTAURANT. WE HAVE THE BEST DOG FOOD IN TOWN.
MENU

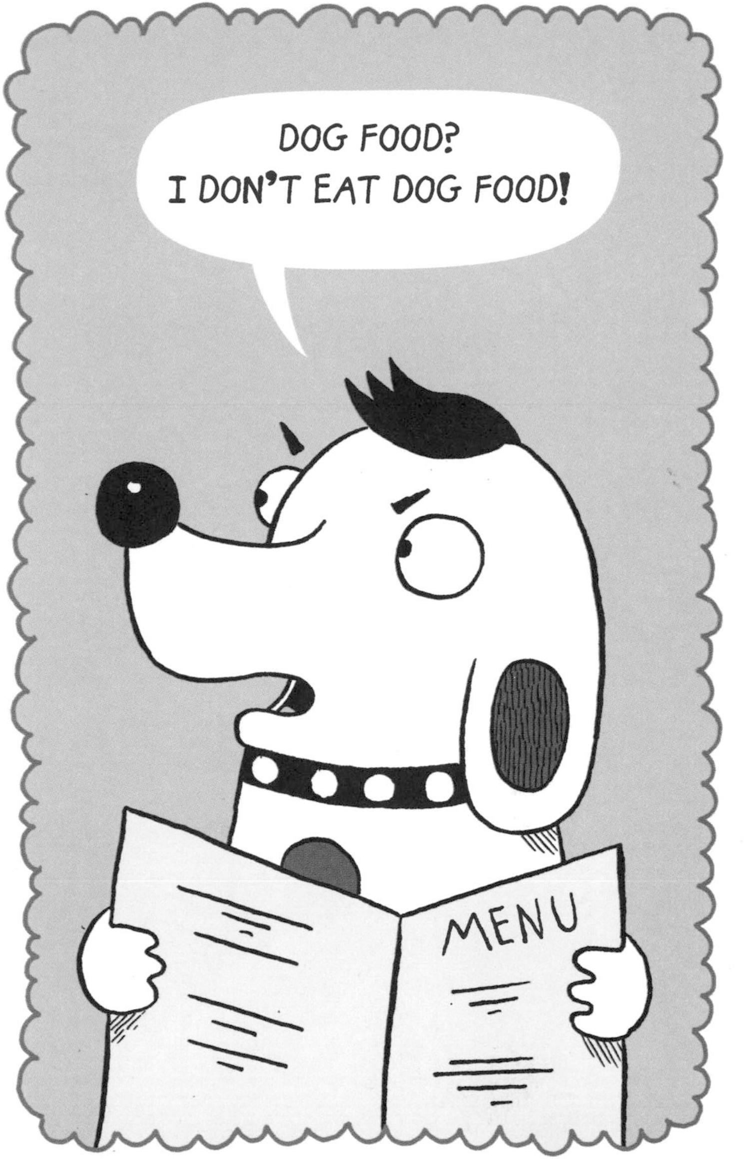
DOG FOOD? I DON'T EAT DOG FOOD!
MENU

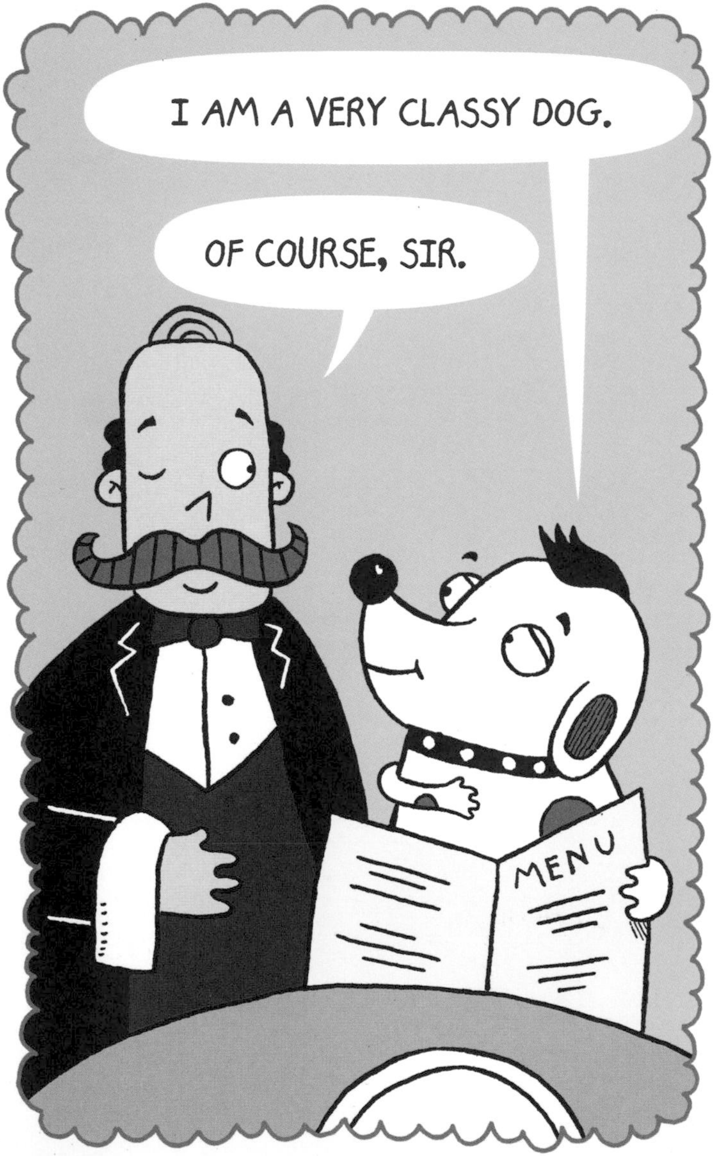
I AM A VERY CLASSY DOG.
OF COURSE, SIR.
MENU

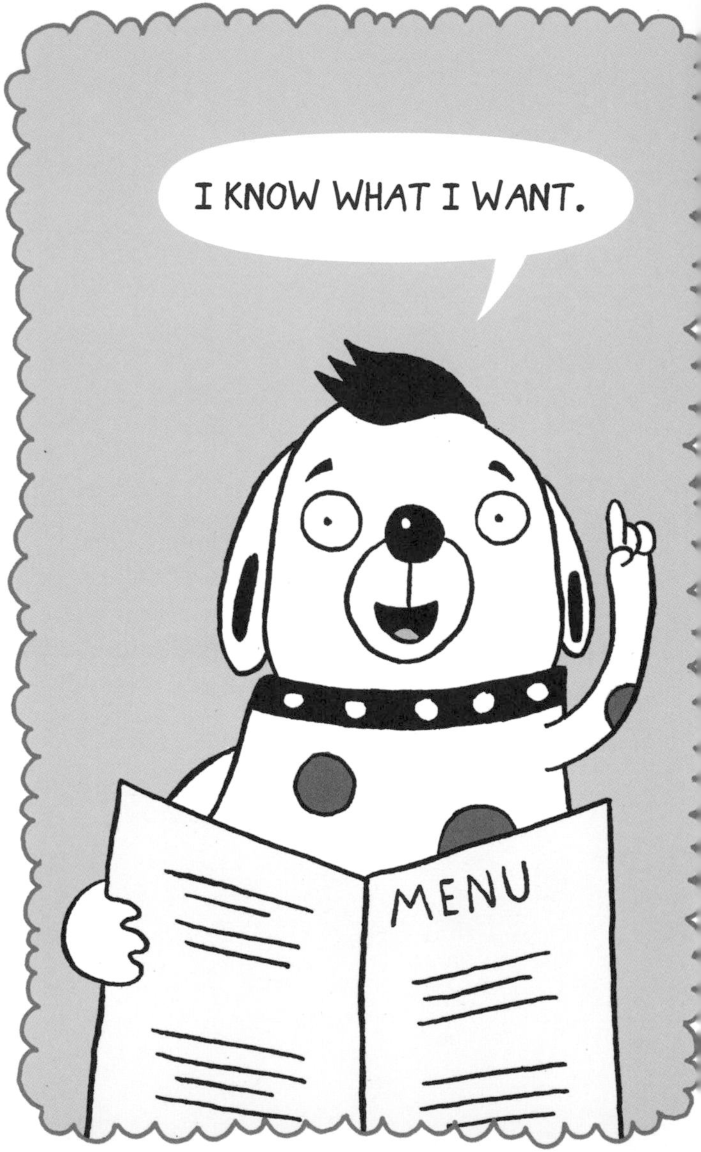
I KNOW WHAT I WANT.
MENU

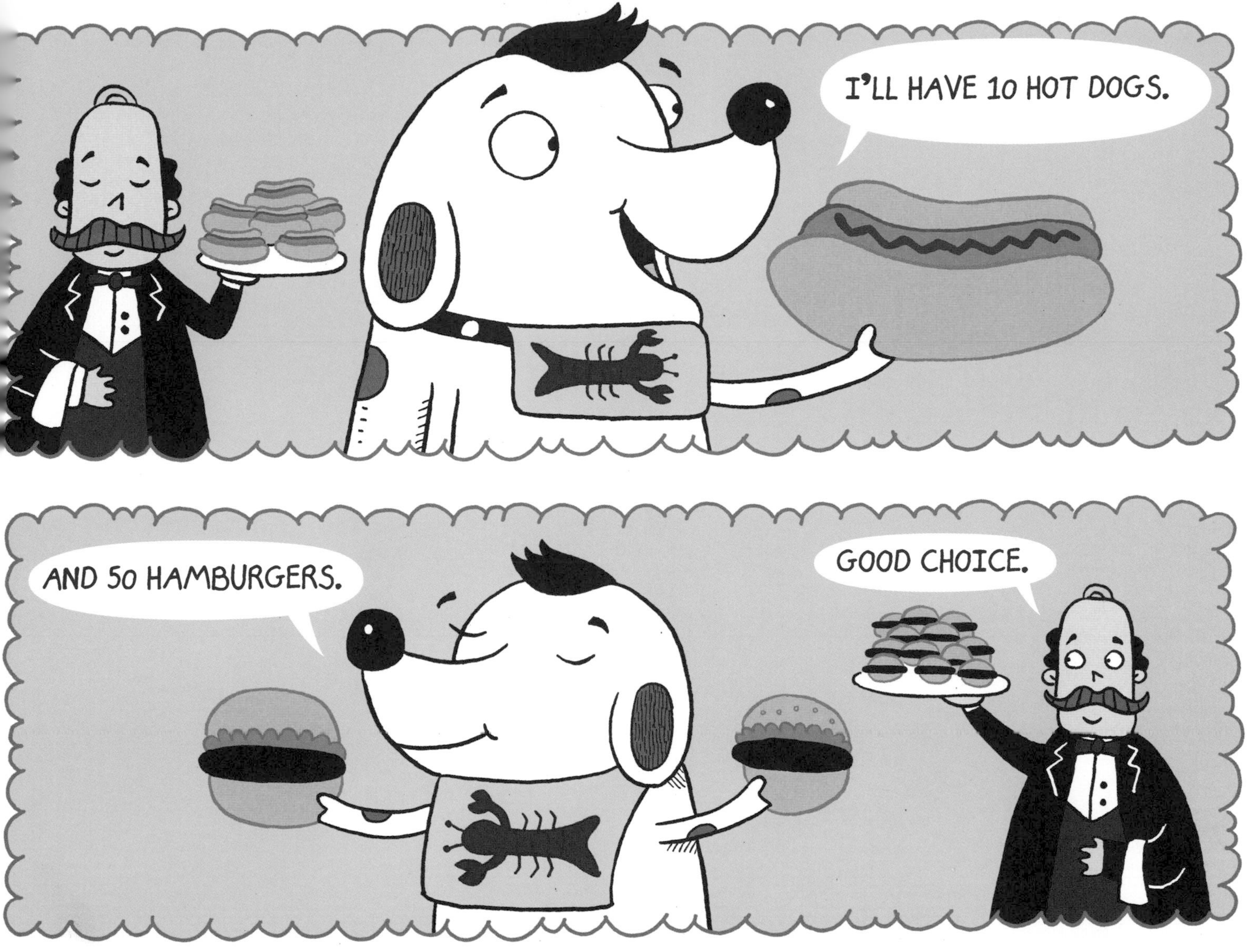
I'LL HAVE 10 HOT DOGS.
AND 50 HAMBURGERS.
GOOD CHOICE.

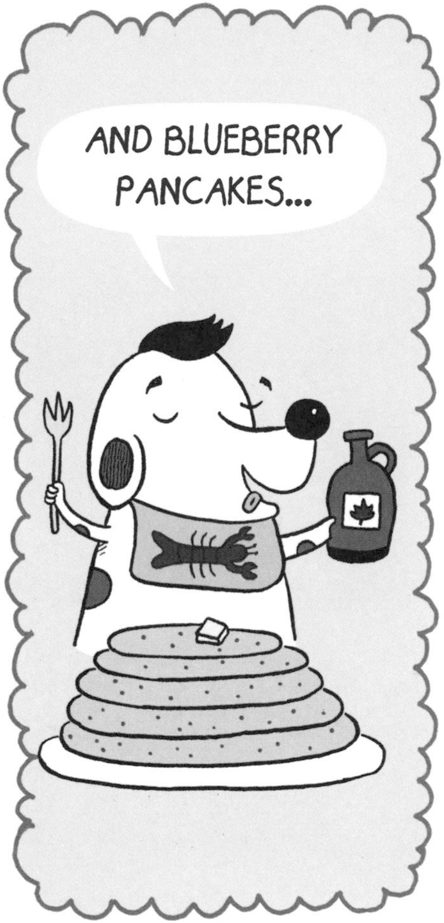
AND BLUEBERRY PANCAKES...

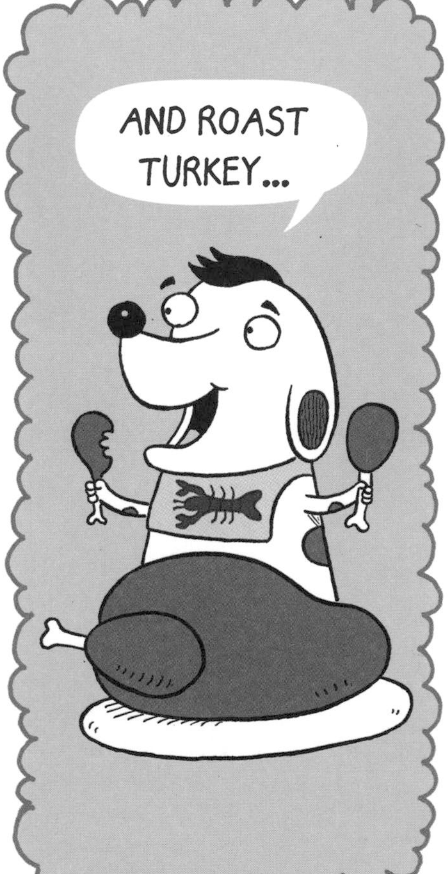
AND ROAST TURKEY...

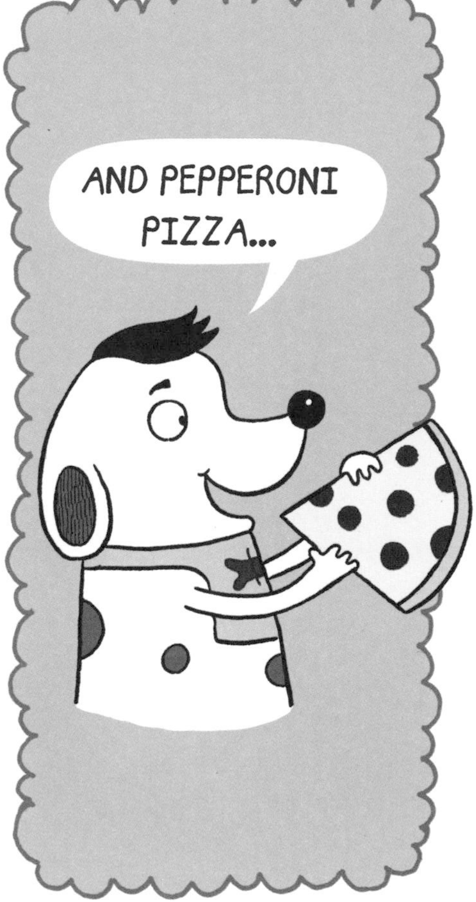
AND PEPPERONI PIZZA...

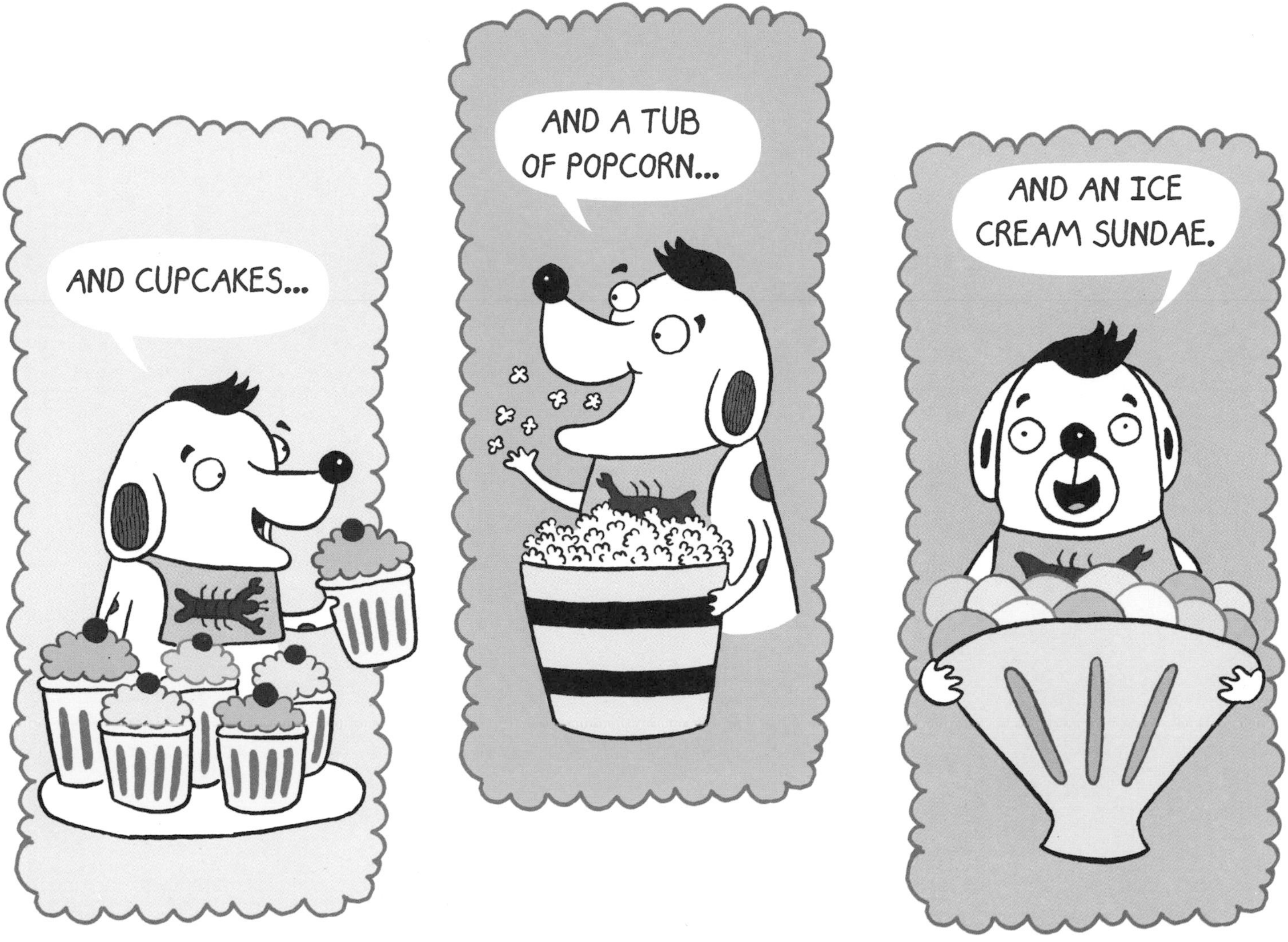
AND CUPCAKES...
AND A TUB OF POPCORN...
AND AN ICE CREAM SUNDAE.

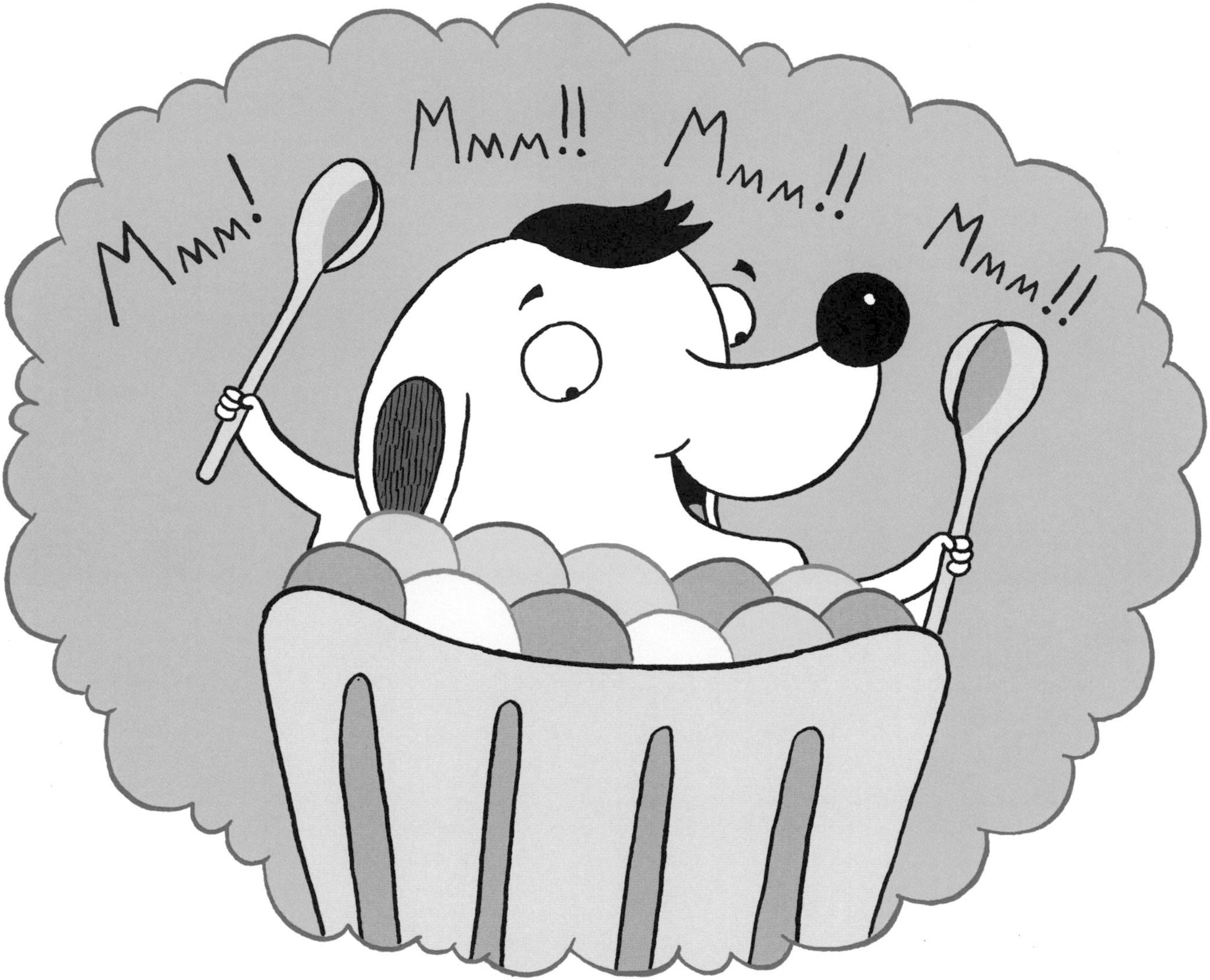
Mmm!
Mmm!!
Mmm!!
Mmm!!

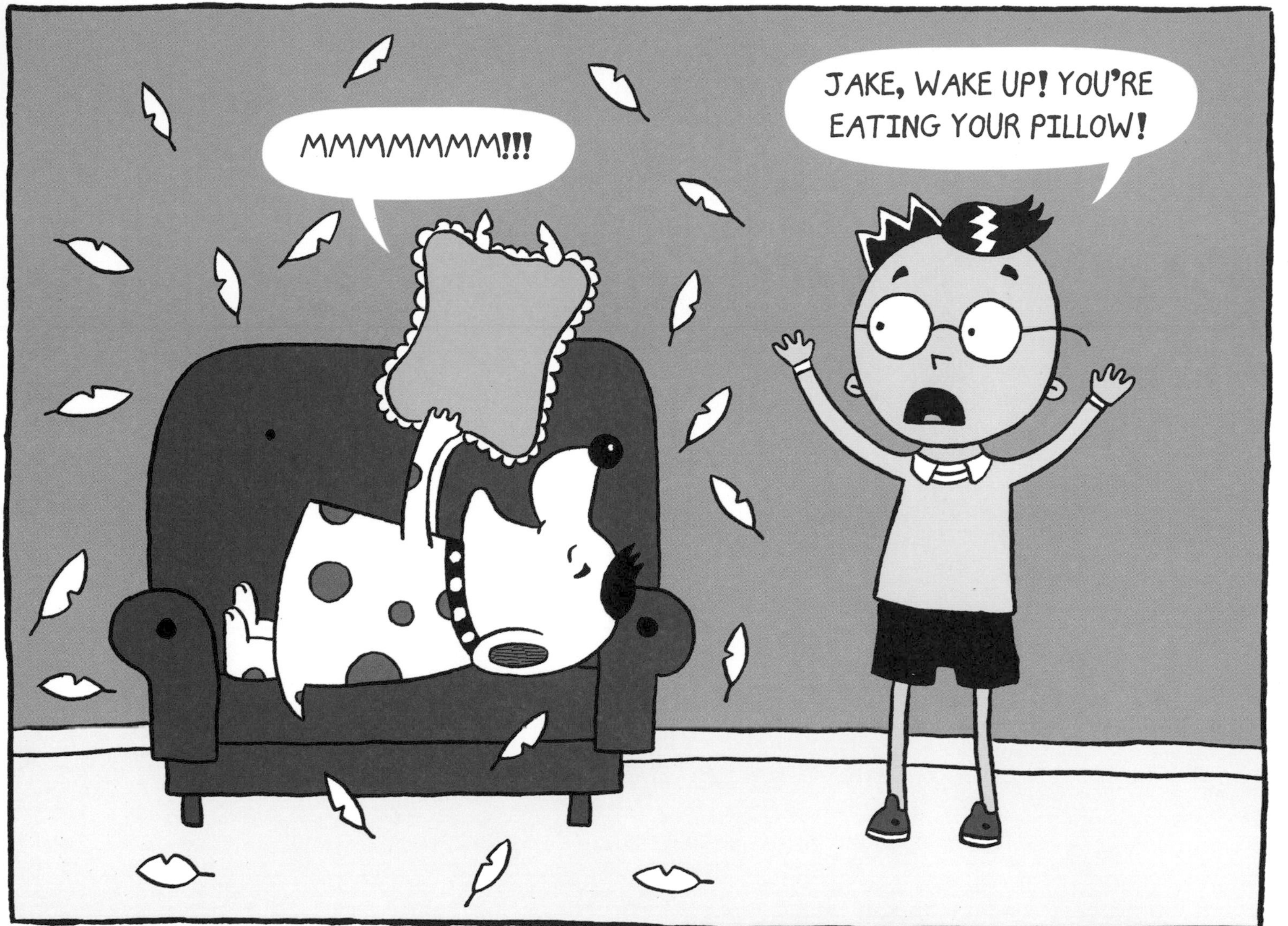
MMMMMMMM!!!
JAKE, WAKE UP! YOU'RE EATING YOUR PILLOW!

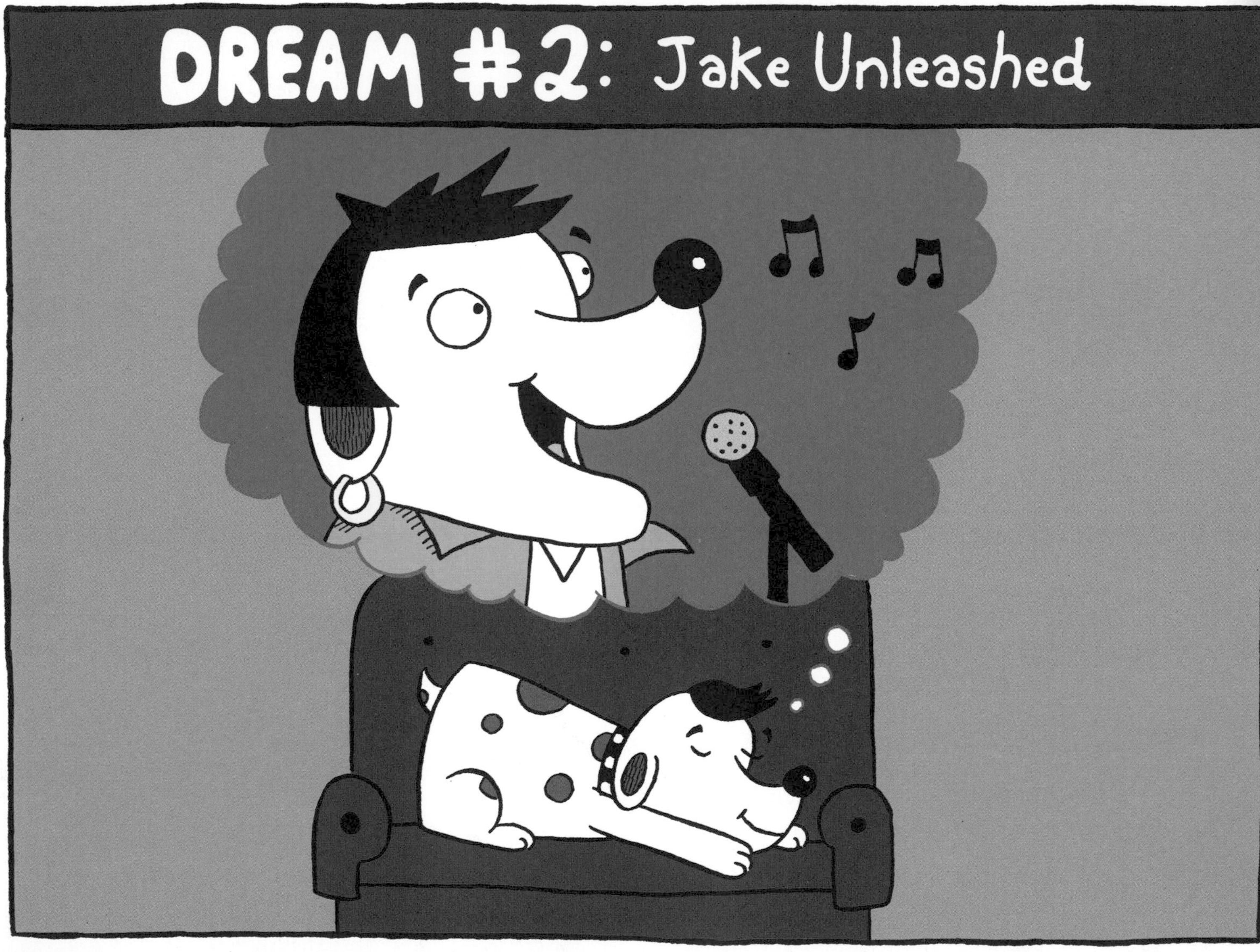
DREAM #2: Jake Unleashed

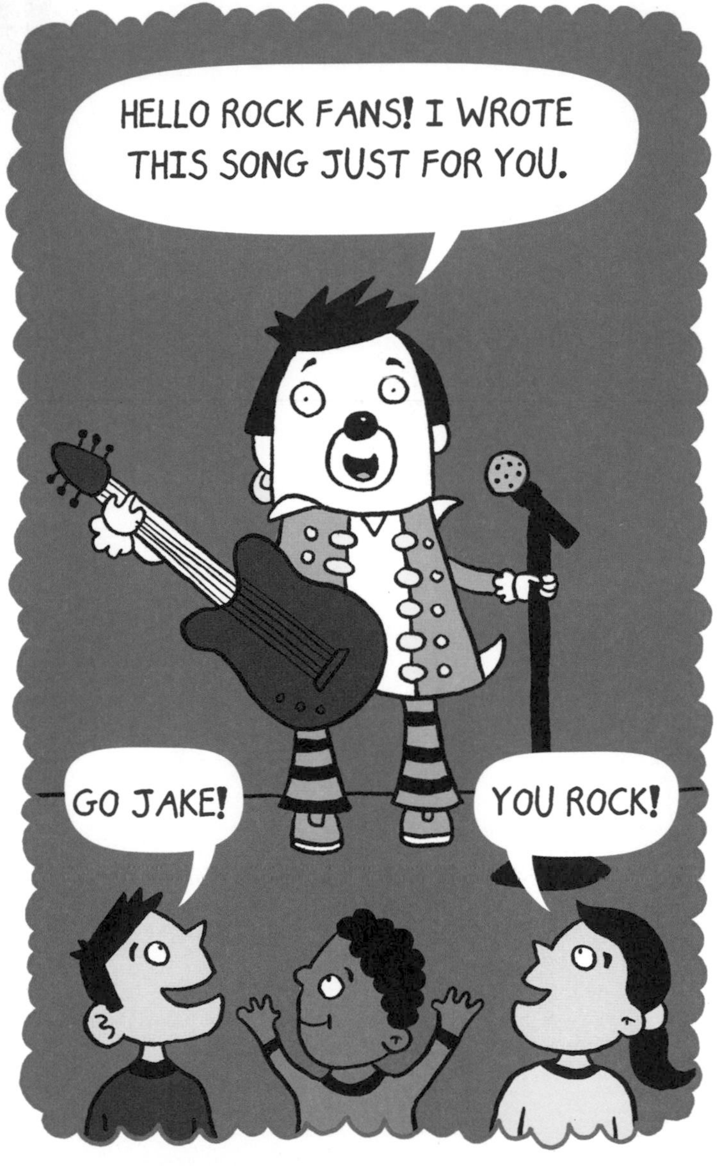
HELLO ROCK FANS! I WROTE THIS SONG JUST FOR YOU.
GO JAKE!
YOU ROCK!

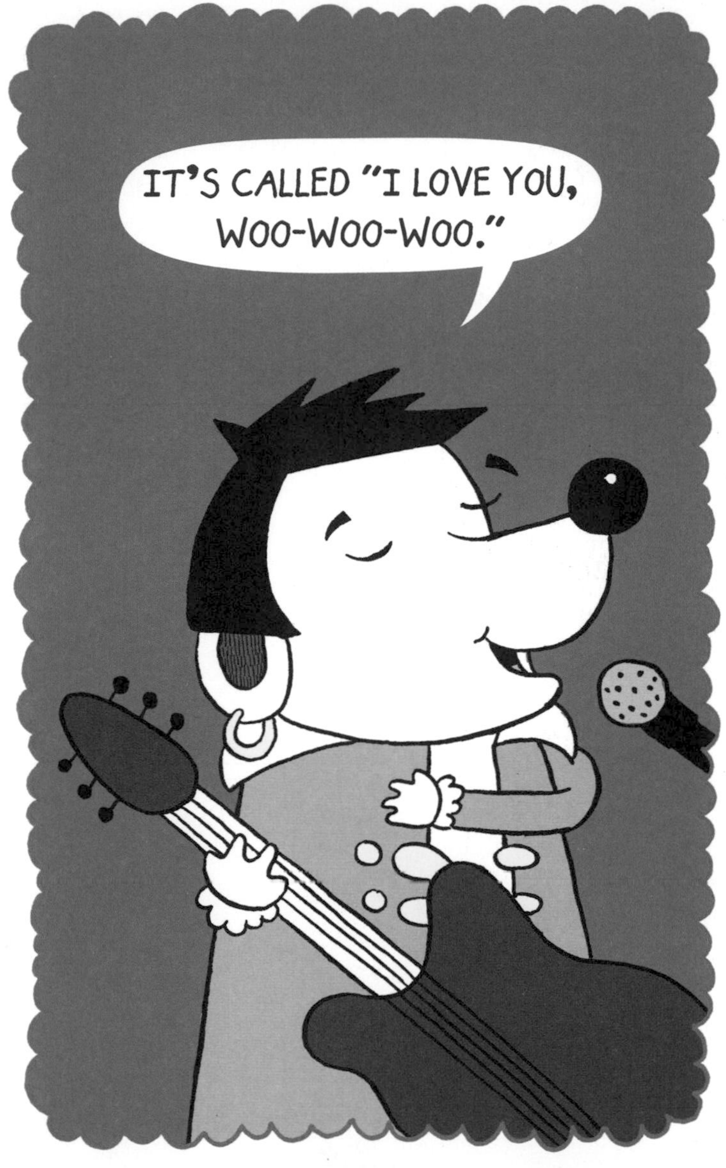
IT'S CALLED "I LOVE YOU, WOO-WOO-WOO."

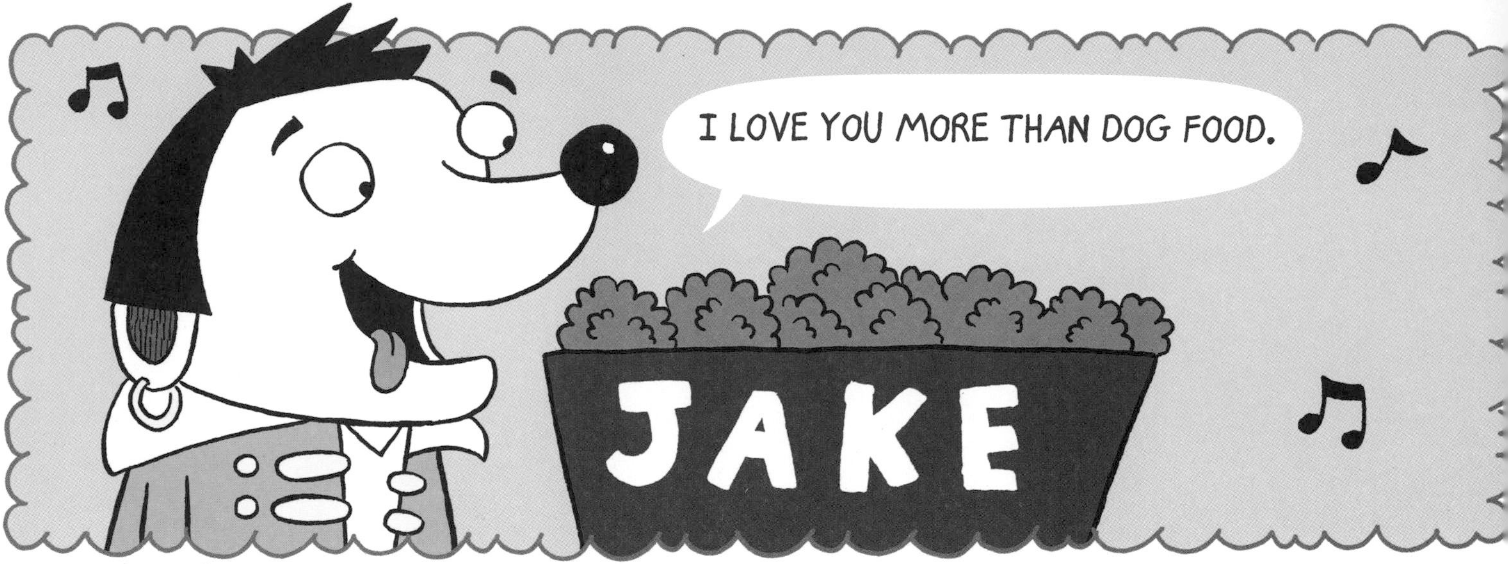
I LOVE YOU MORE THAN DOG FOOD.
JAKE

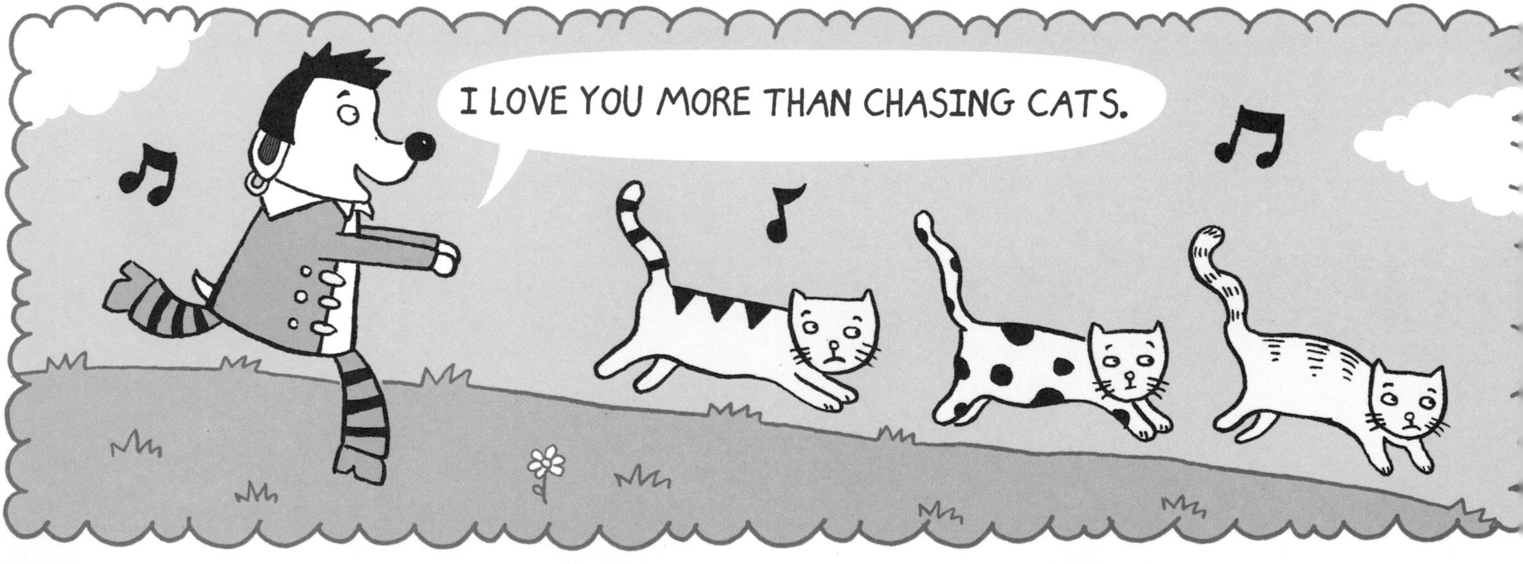
I LOVE YOU MORE THAN CHASING CATS.

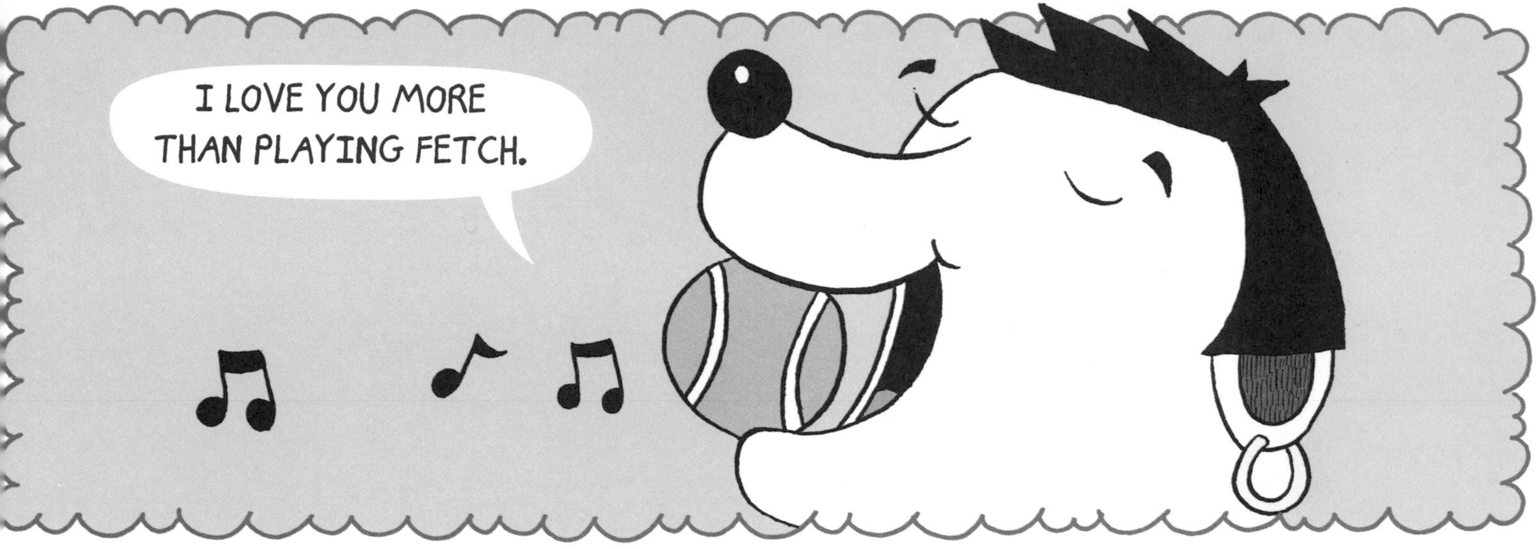
I LOVE YOU MORE
THAN PLAYING FETCH.

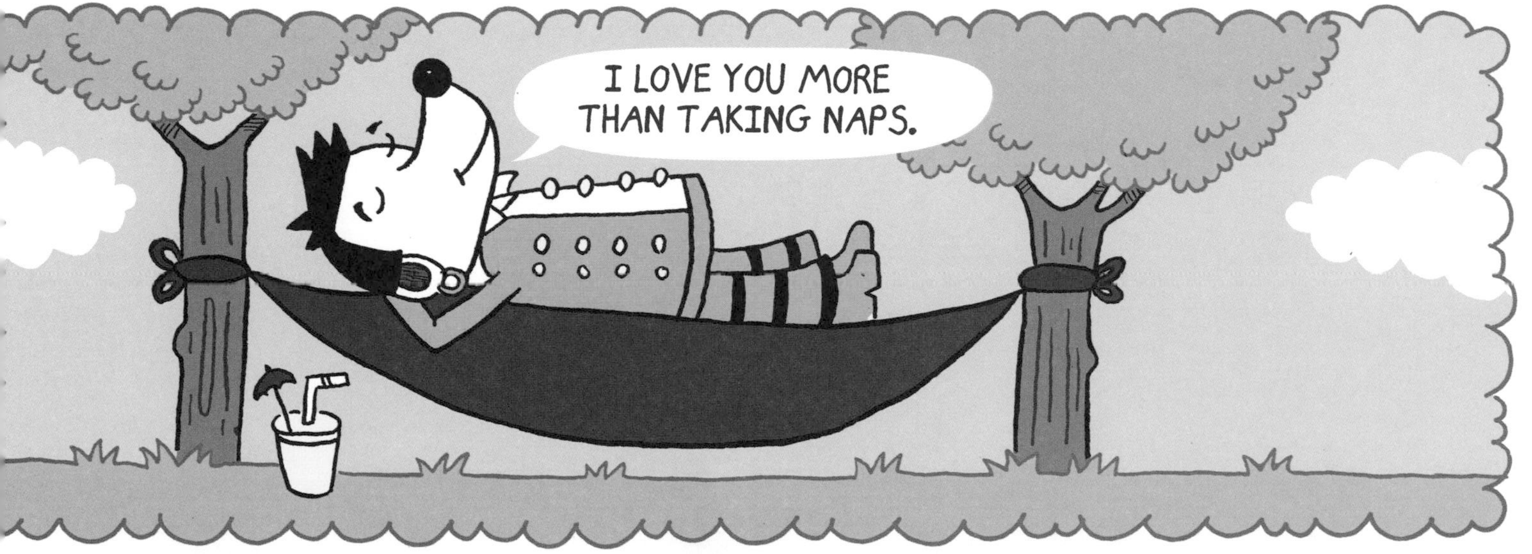
I LOVE YOU MORE
THAN TAKING NAPS.

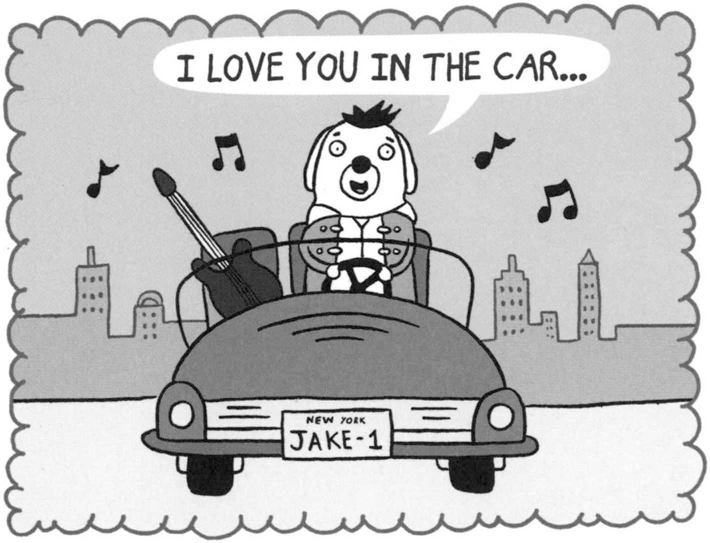
I LOVE YOU IN THE CAR...
NEW YORK
JAKE-1

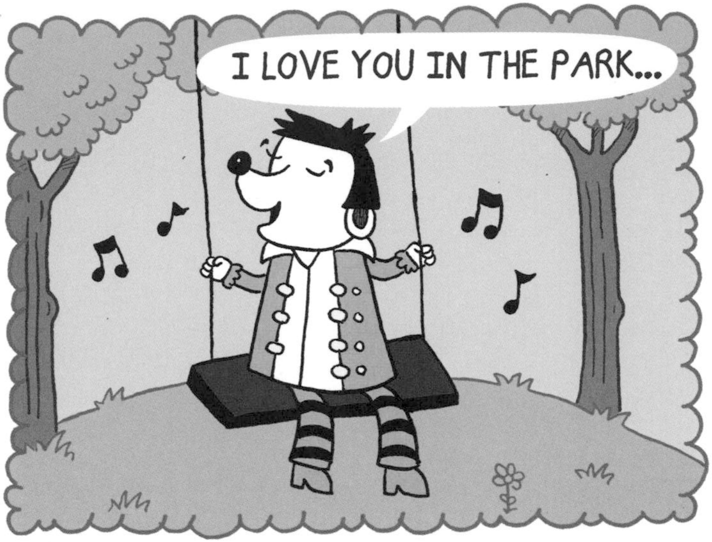
I LOVE YOU IN THE PARK...

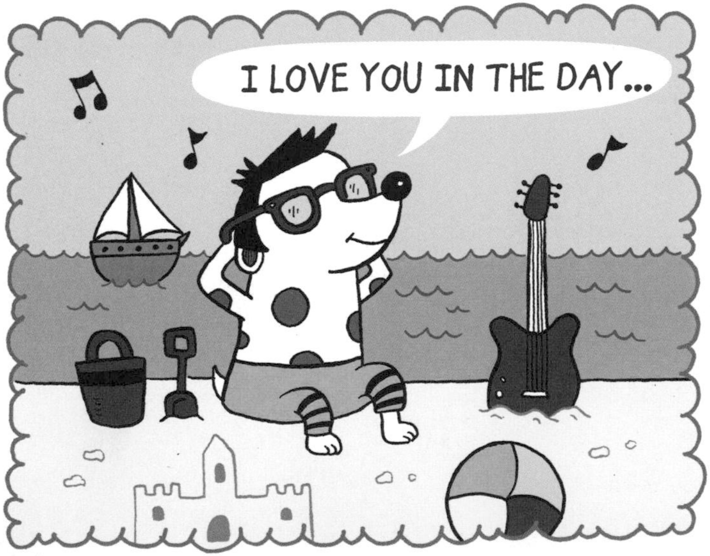
I LOVE YOU IN THE DAY...

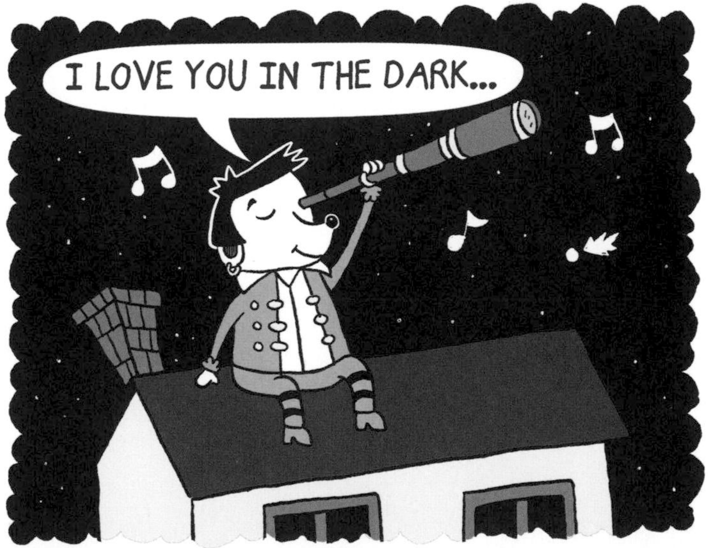
I LOVE YOU IN THE DARK...

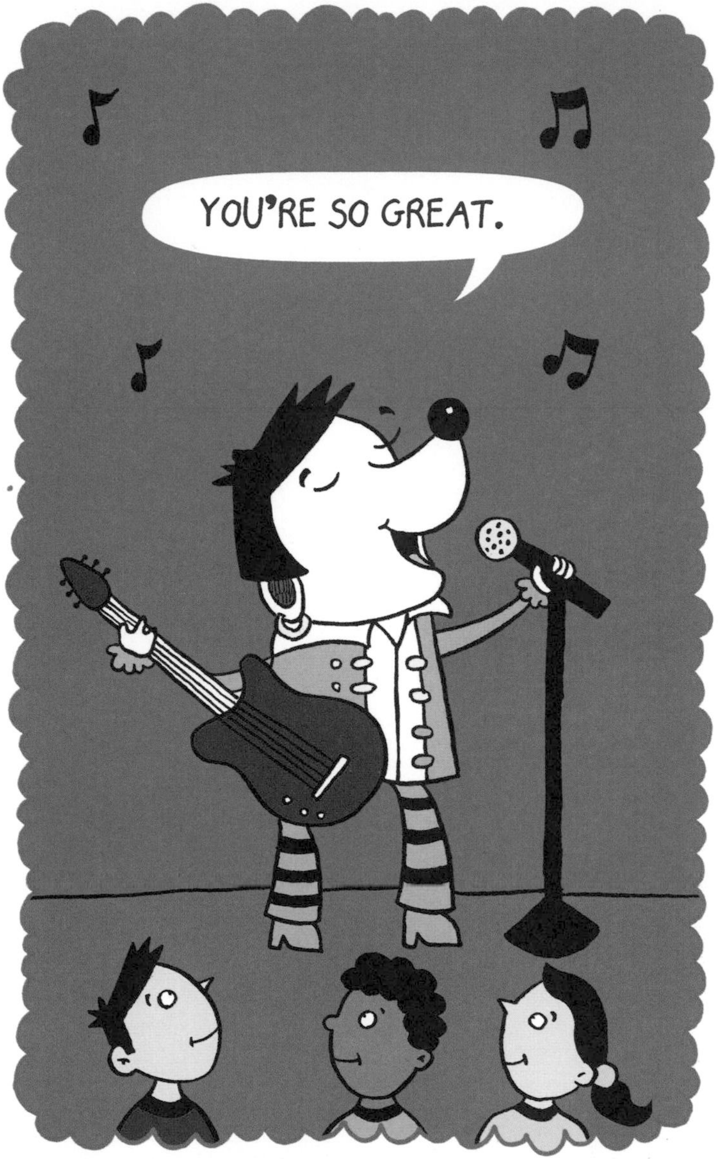
YOU'RE SO GREAT.

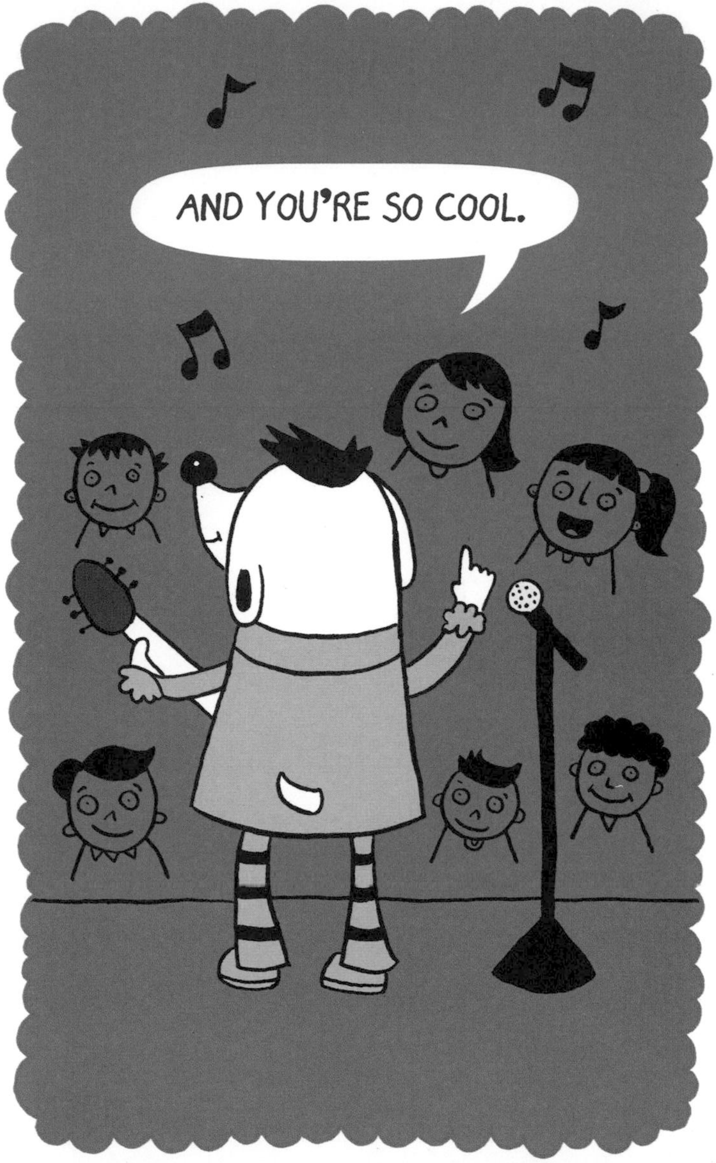
AND YOU'RE SO COOL.

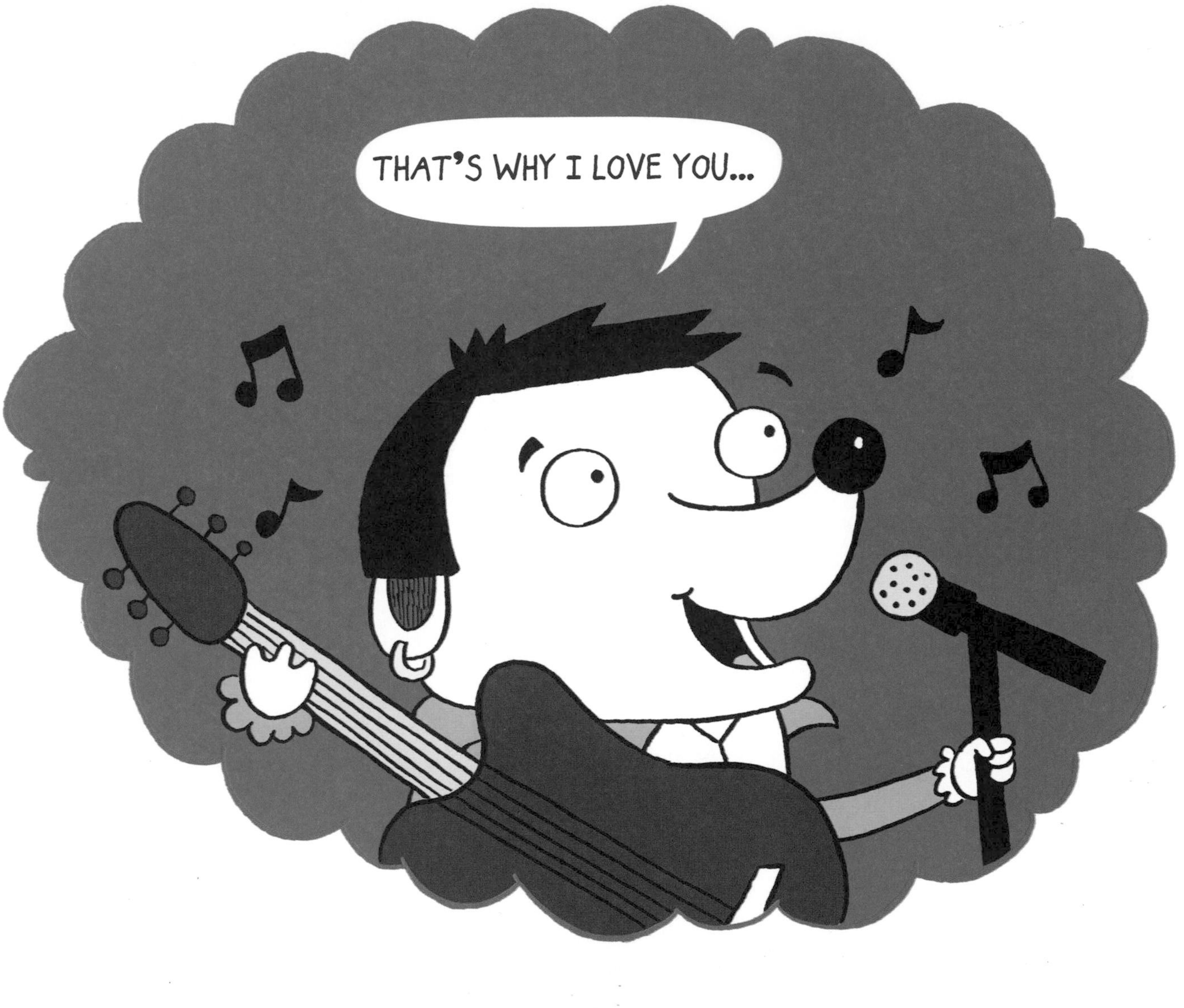
THAT'S WHY I LOVE YOU...

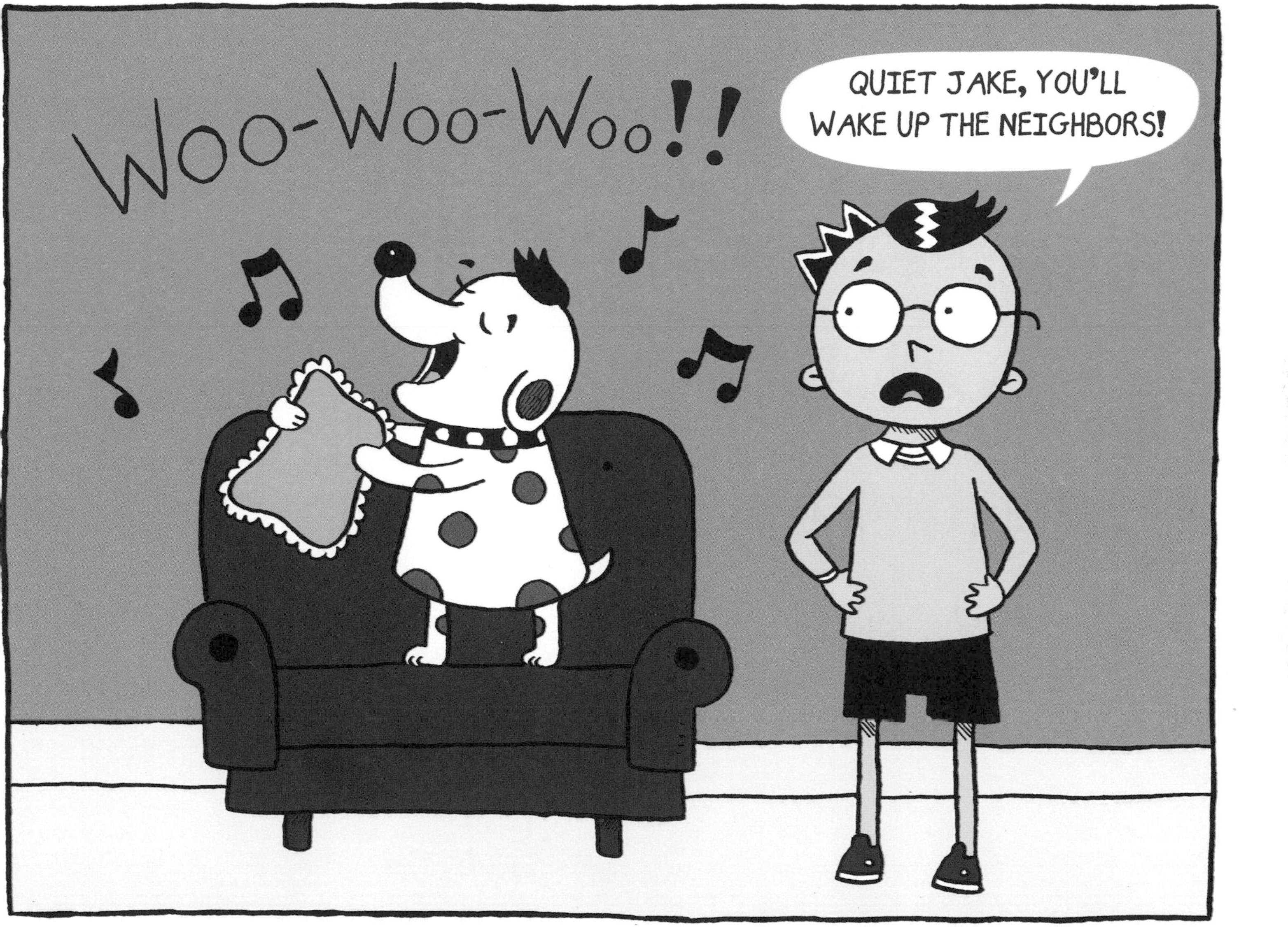
Woo-Woo-Woo!!
QUIET JAKE, YOU'LL WAKE UP THE NEIGHBORS!

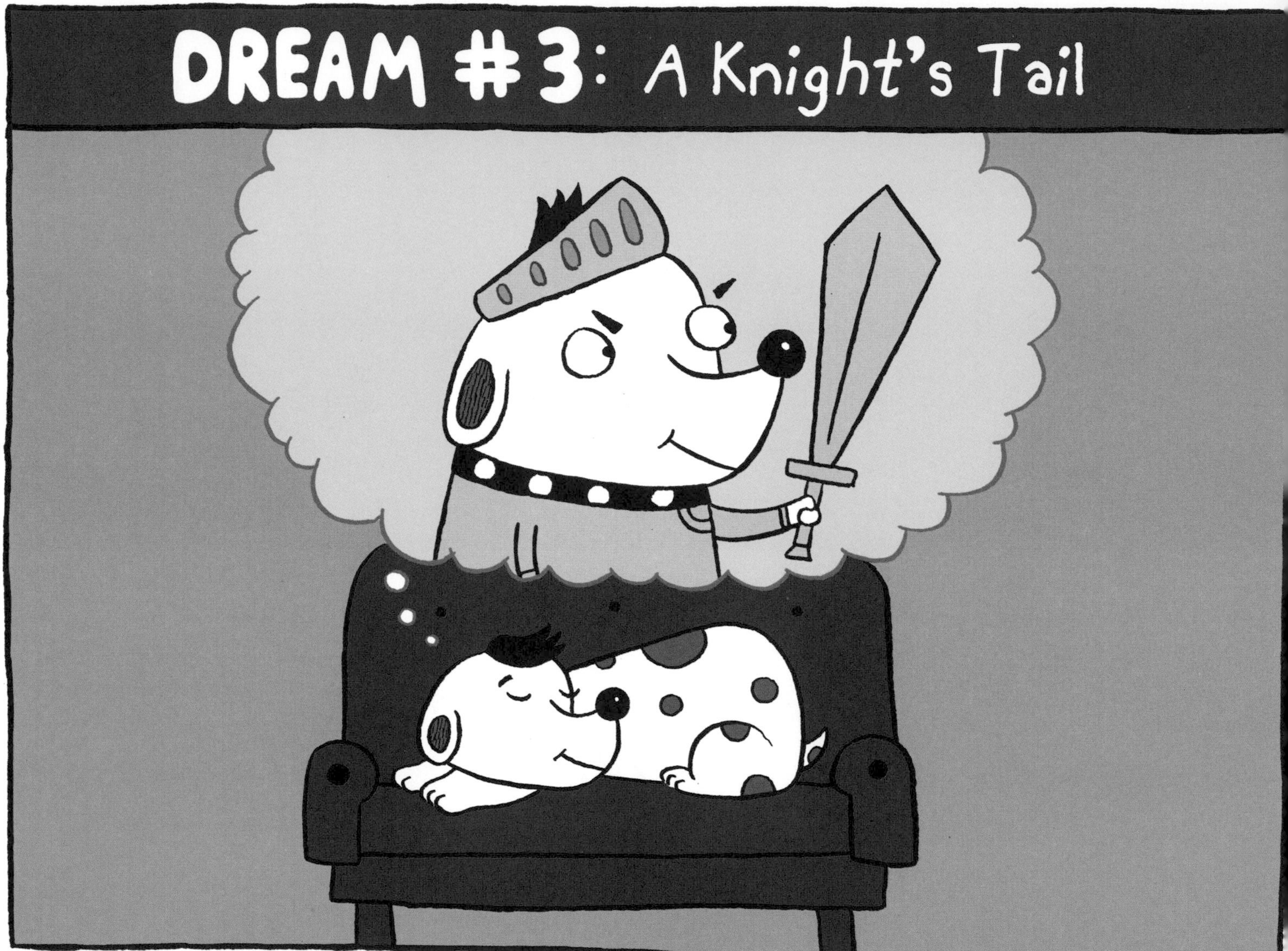
DREAM #3: A Knight's Tail

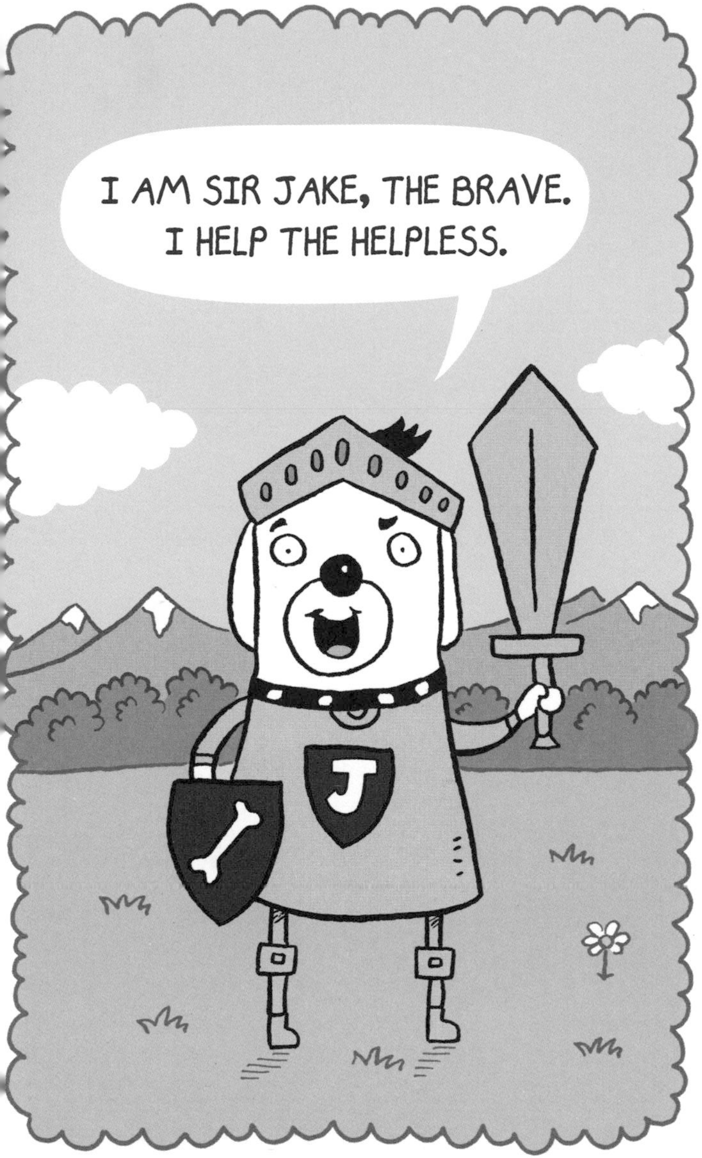
I AM SIR JAKE, THE BRAVE.
I HELP THE HELPLESS.

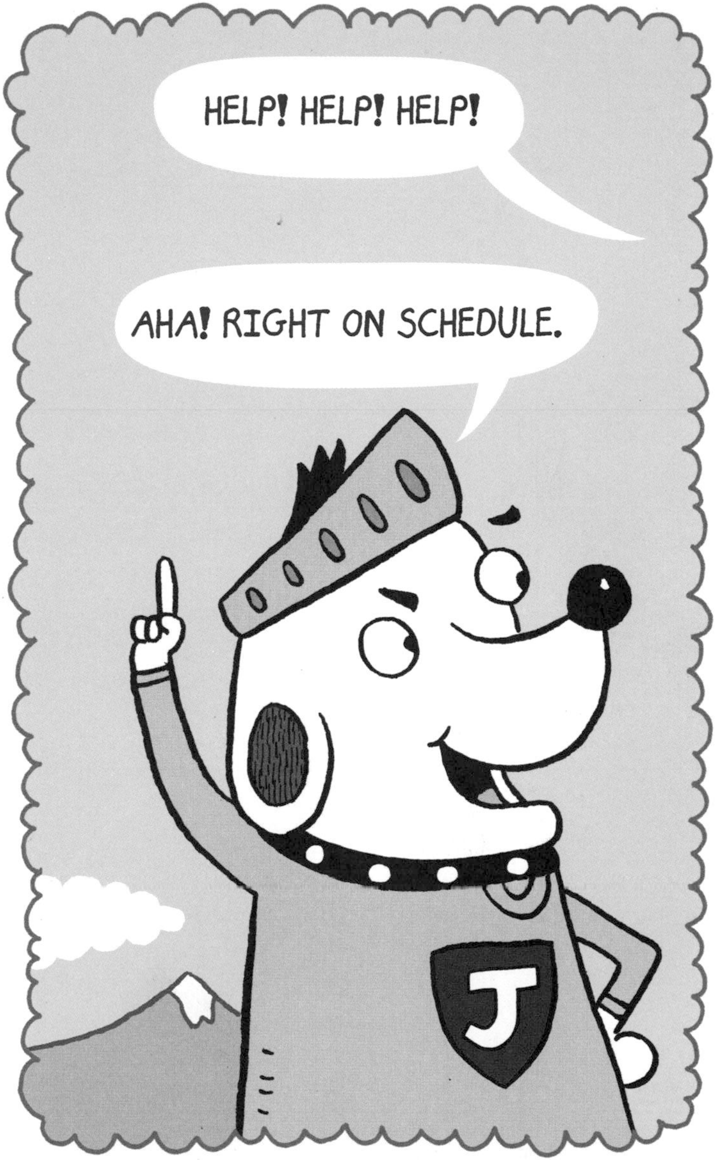
HELP! HELP! HELP!
AHA! RIGHT ON SCHEDULE.

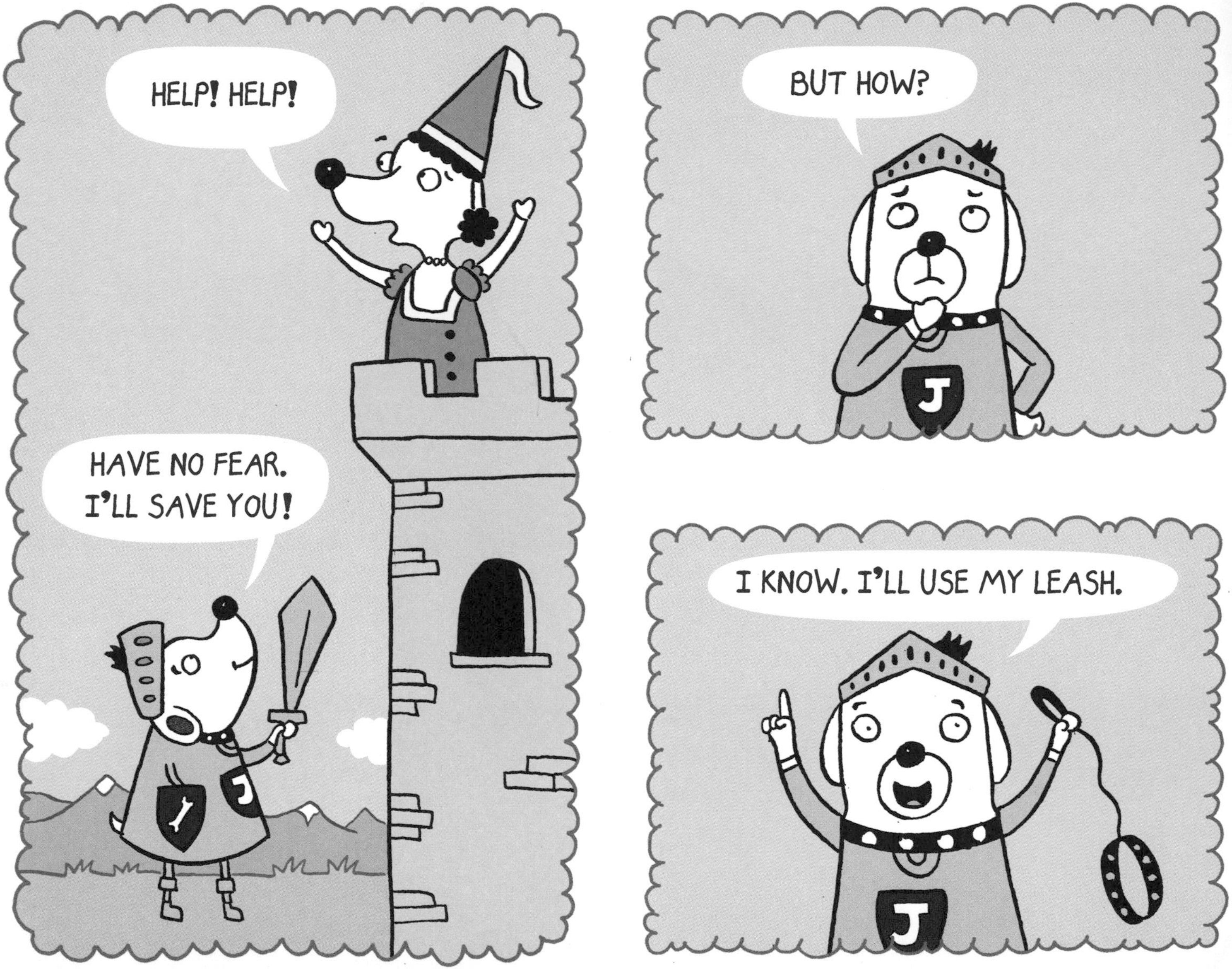
HELP! HELP!
HAVE NO FEAR. I'LL SAVE YOU!
BUT HOW?
I KNOW. I'LL USE MY LEASH.

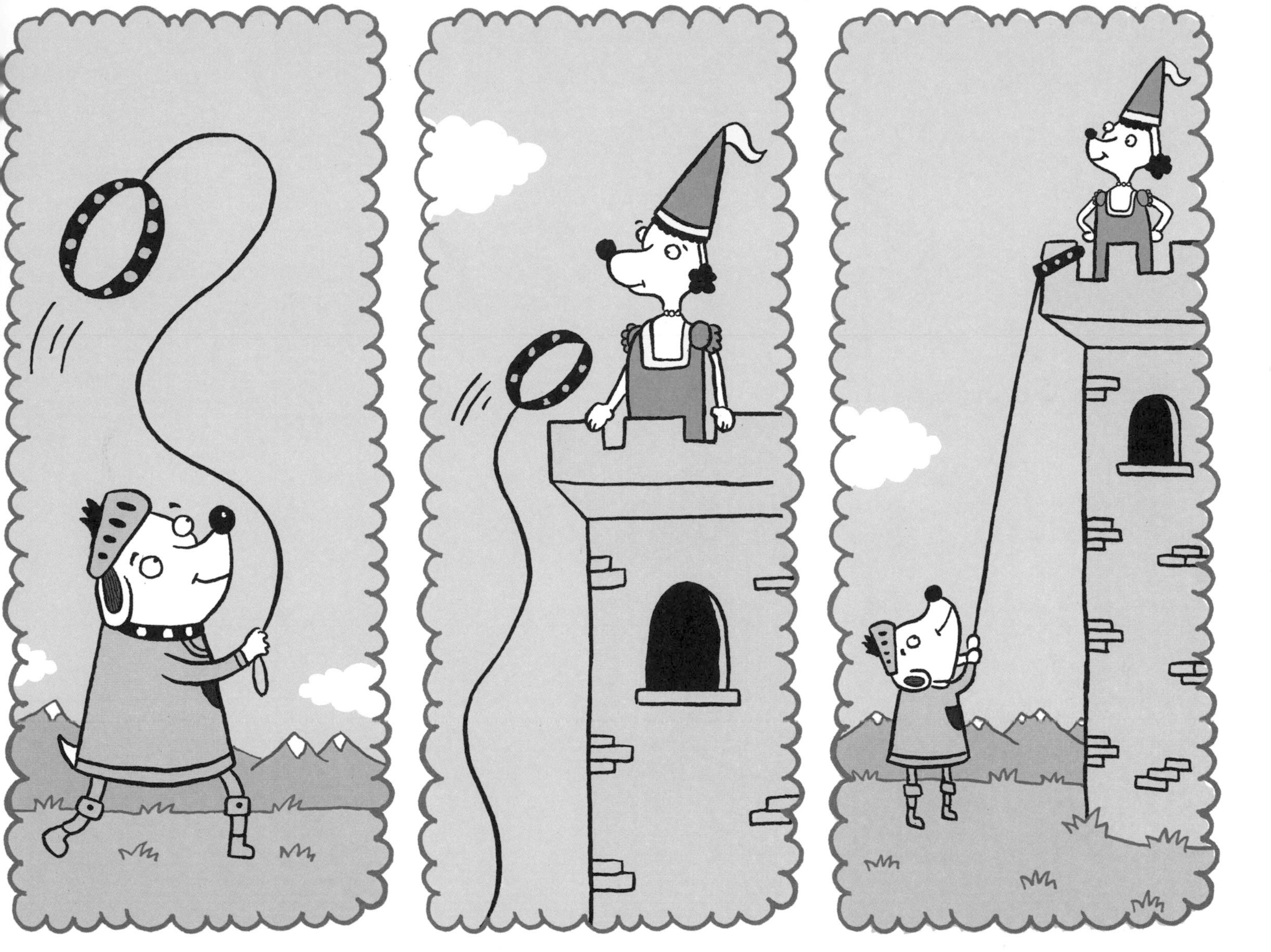

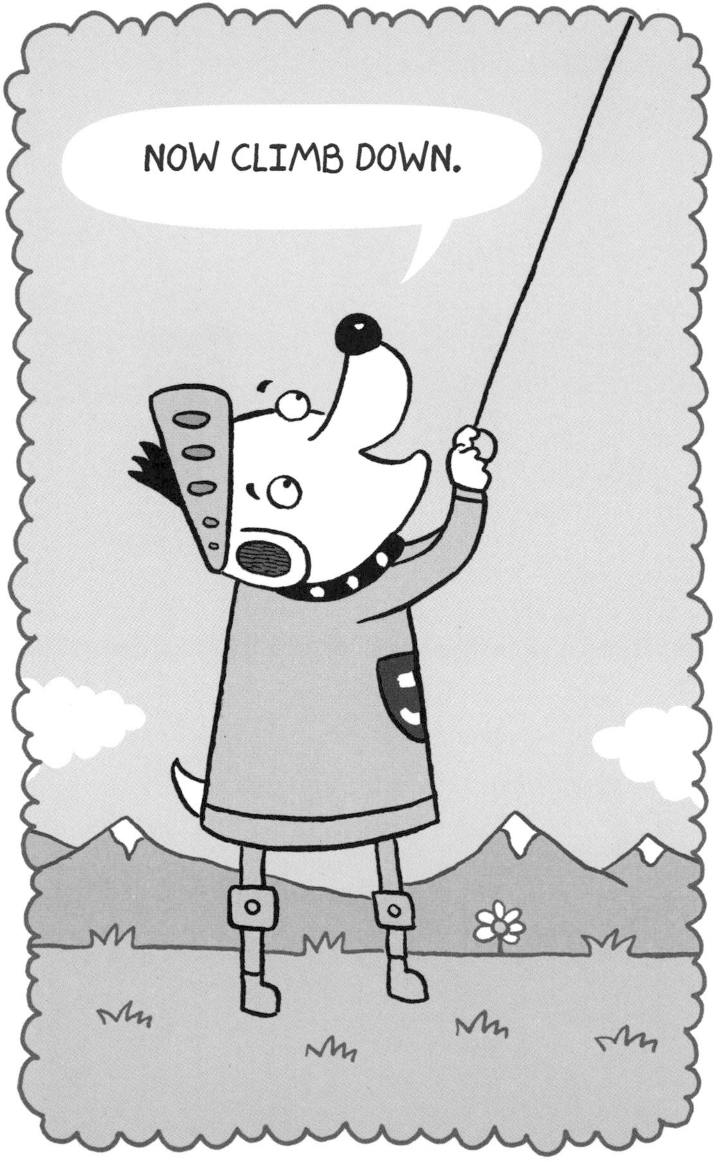
NOW CLIMB DOWN.

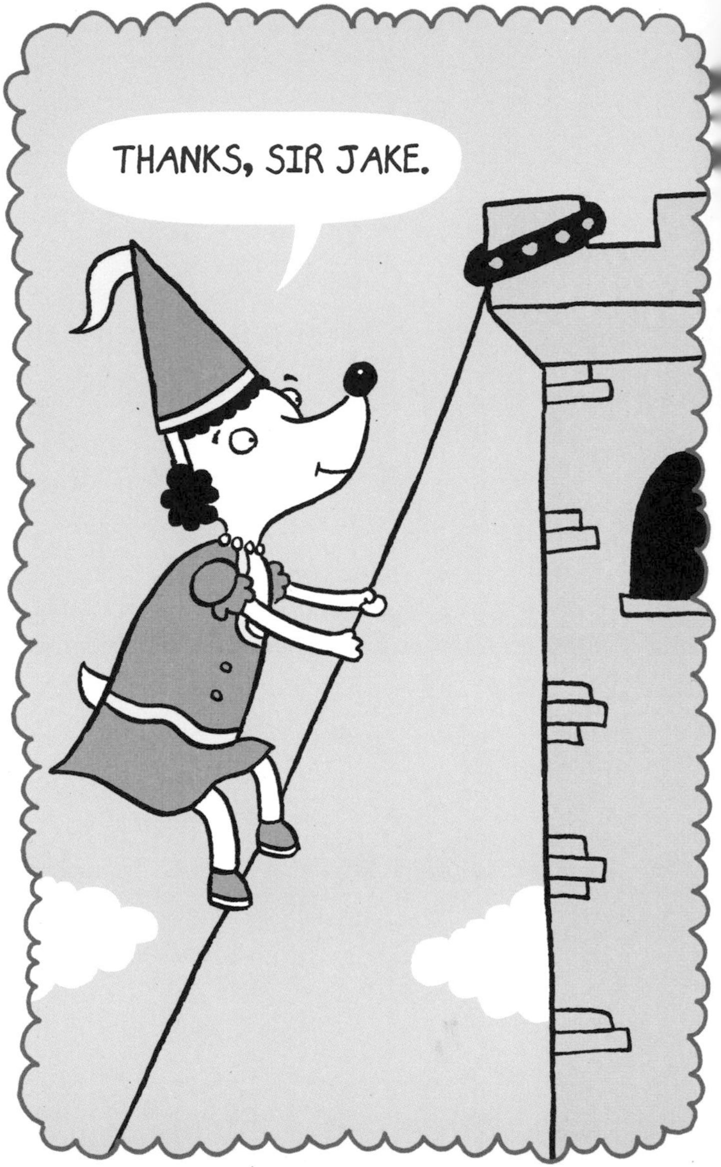
THANKS, SIR JAKE.

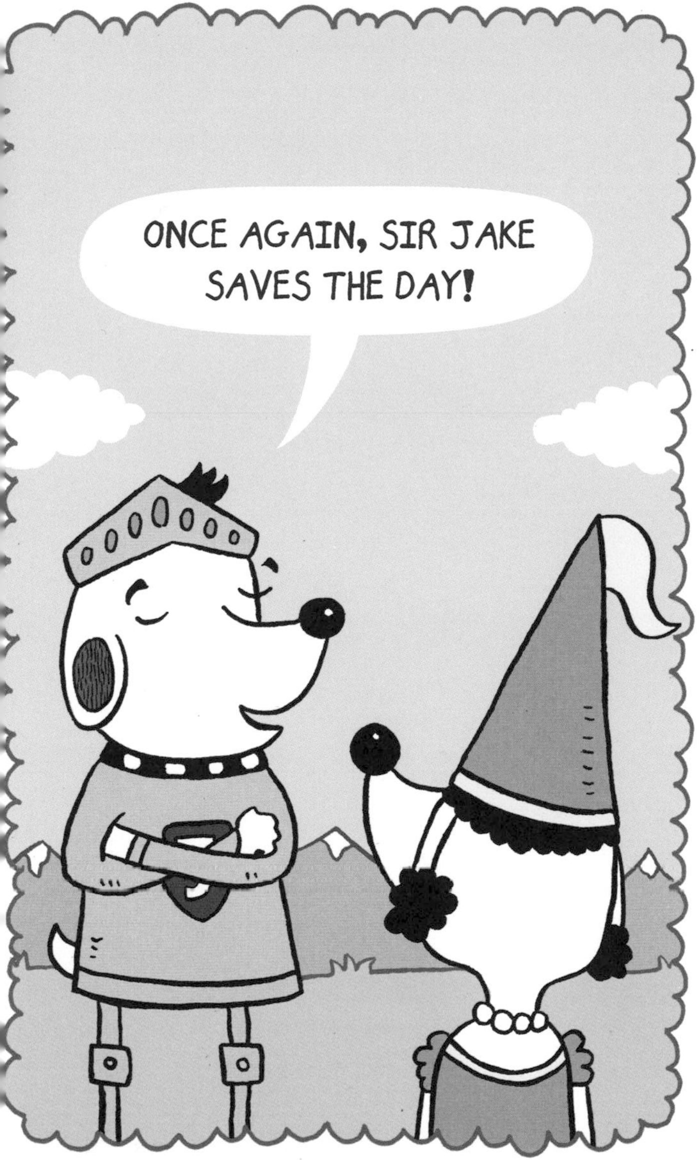
ONCE AGAIN, SIR JAKE SAVES THE DAY!

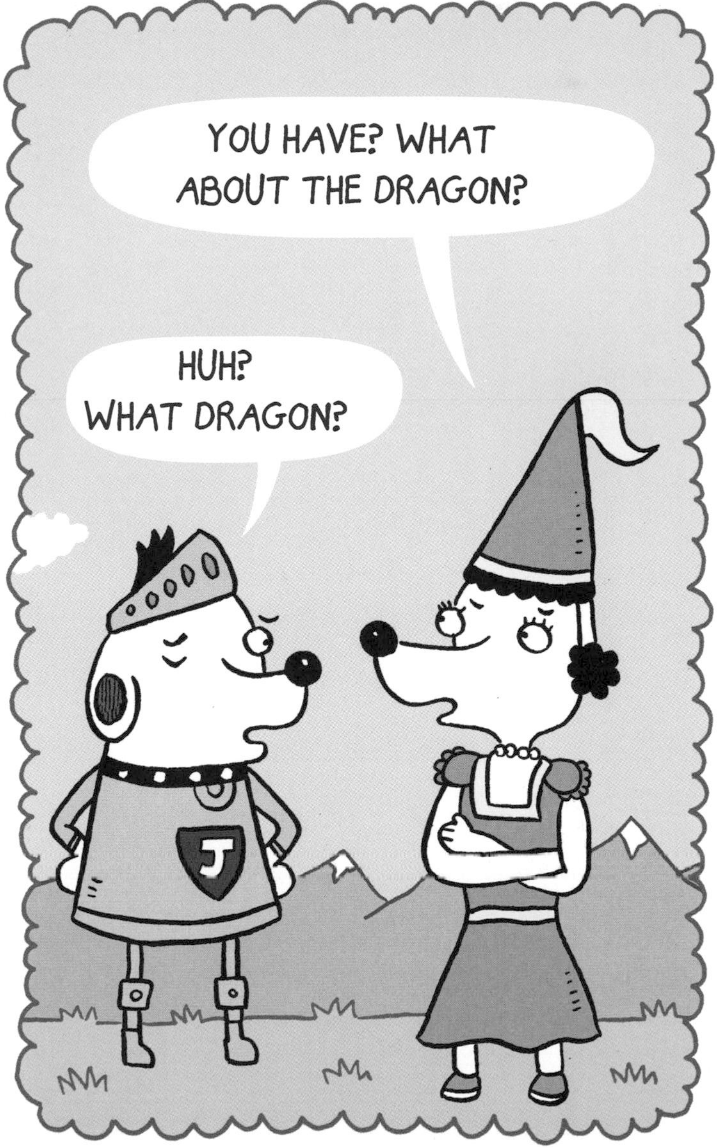
YOU HAVE? WHAT ABOUT THE DRAGON?
HUH? WHAT DRAGON?

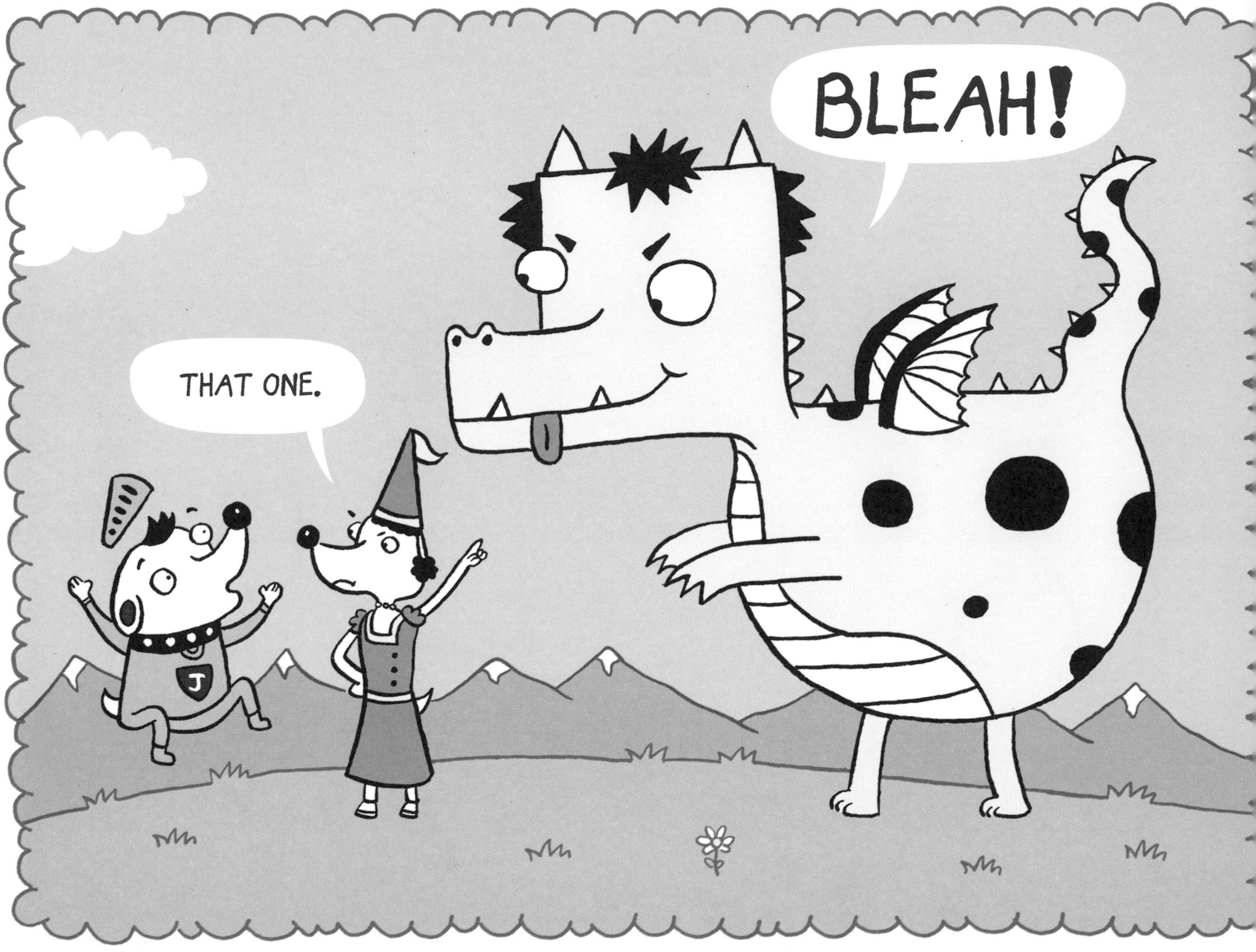
THAT ONE.
BLEAH!

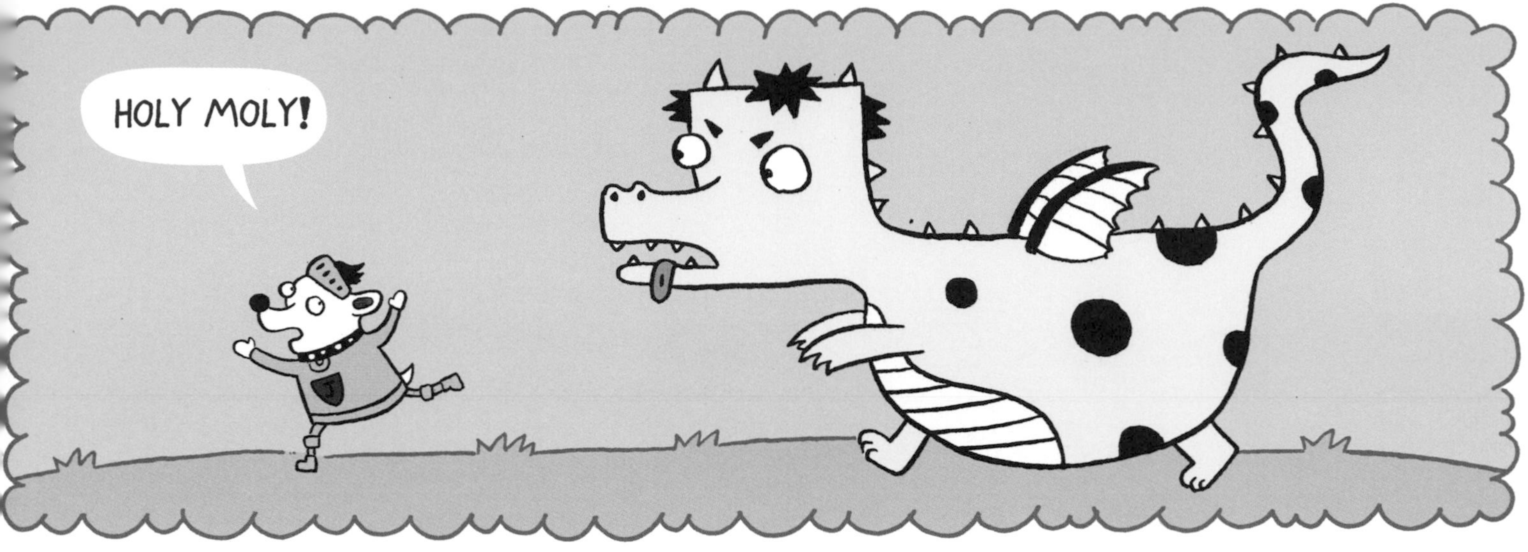
HOLY MOLY!

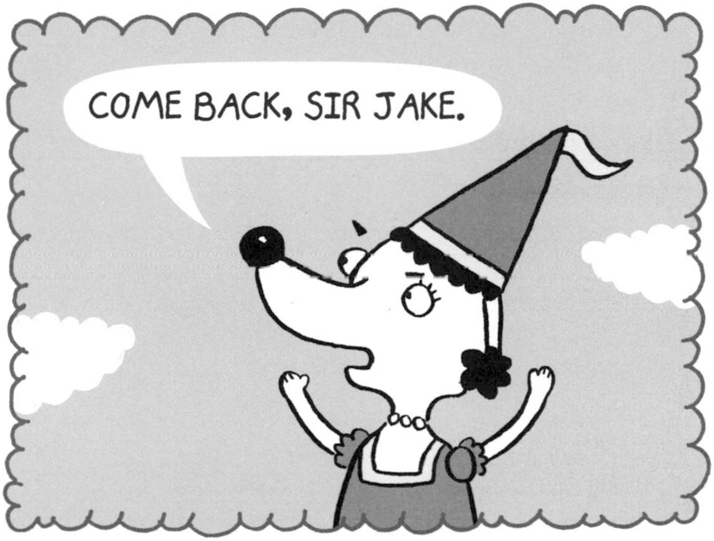
COME BACK, SIR JAKE.

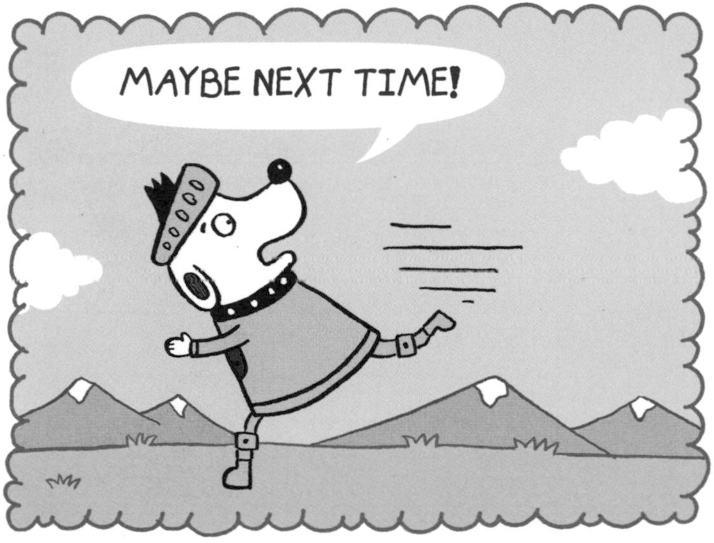
MAYBE NEXT TIME!

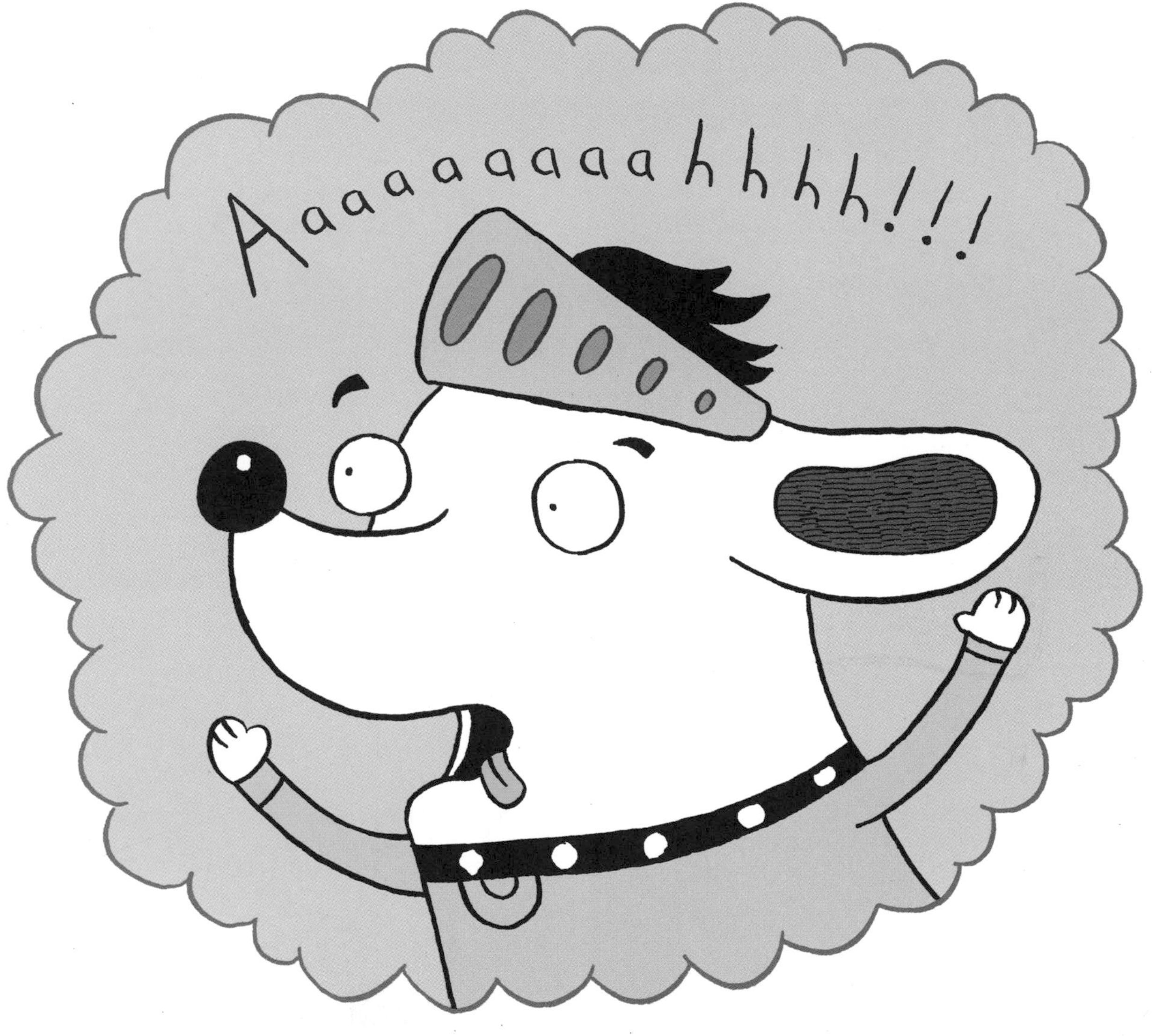
Aaaaaaaaahhhhh!!!!

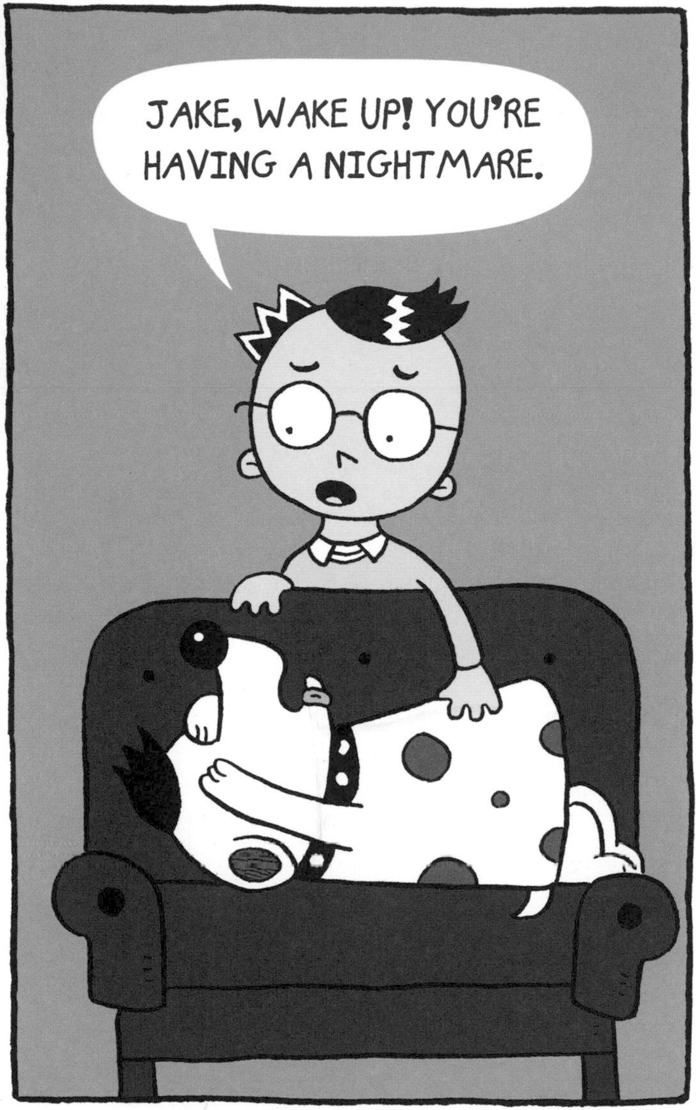
JAKE, WAKE UP! YOU'RE HAVING A NIGHTMARE.

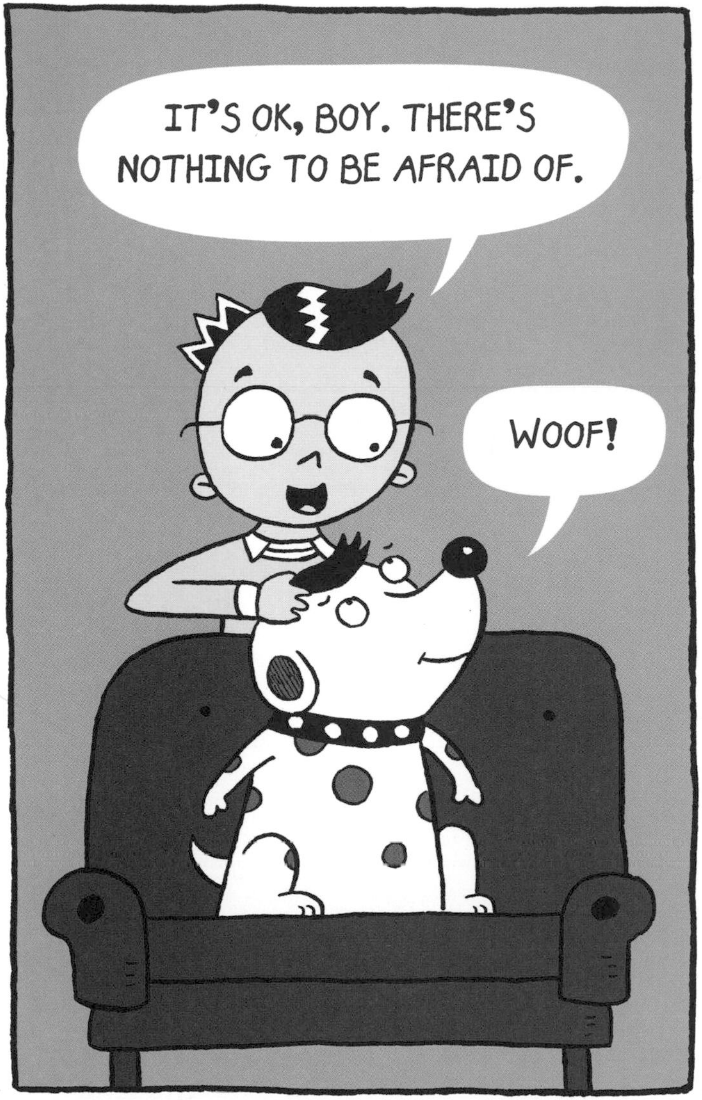
IT'S OK, BOY. THERE'S NOTHING TO BE AFRAID OF.
WOOF!

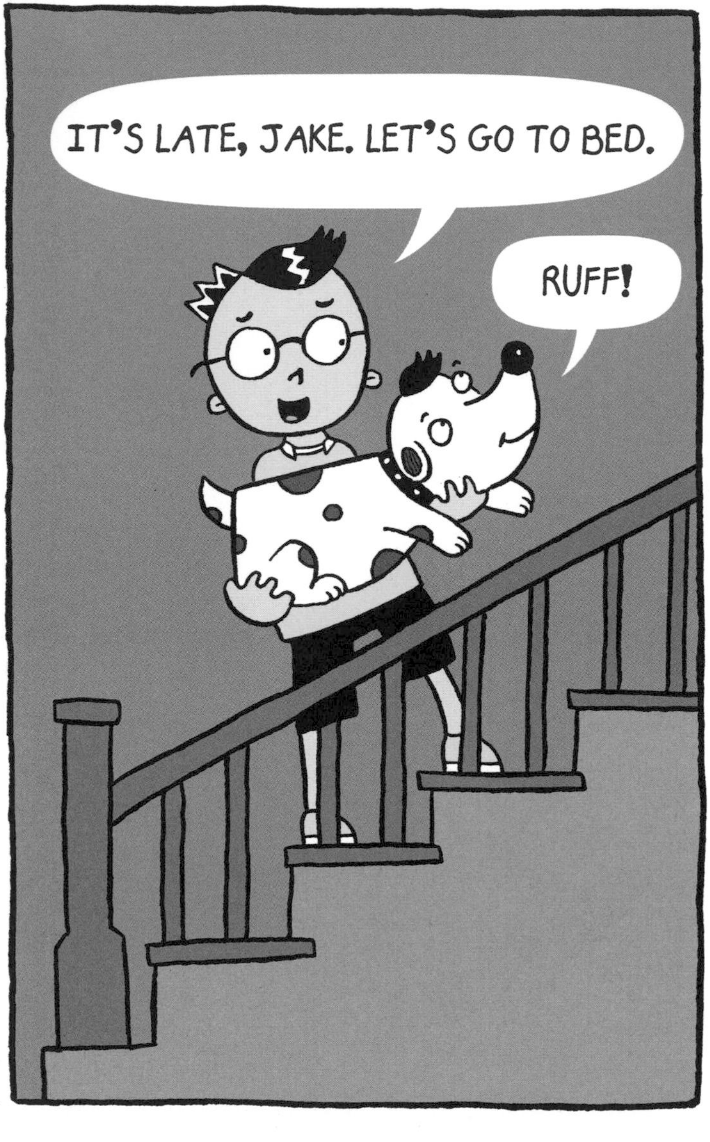
IT'S LATE, JAKE. LET'S GO TO BED.
RUFF!

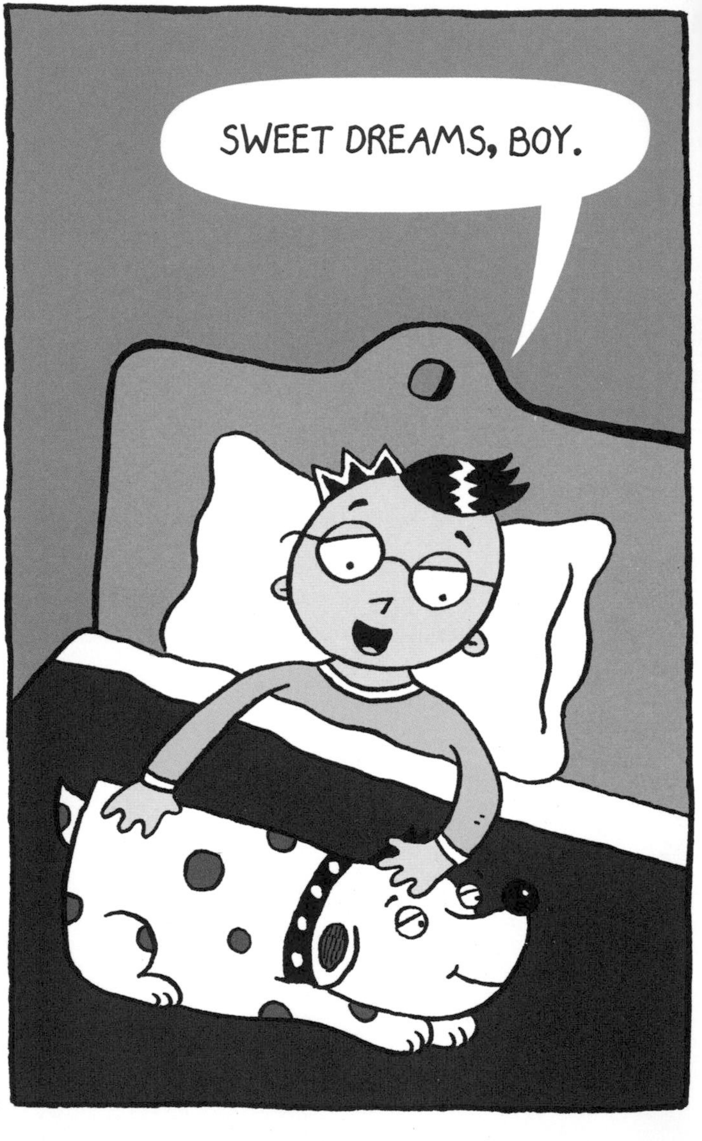
SWEET DREAMS, BOY.

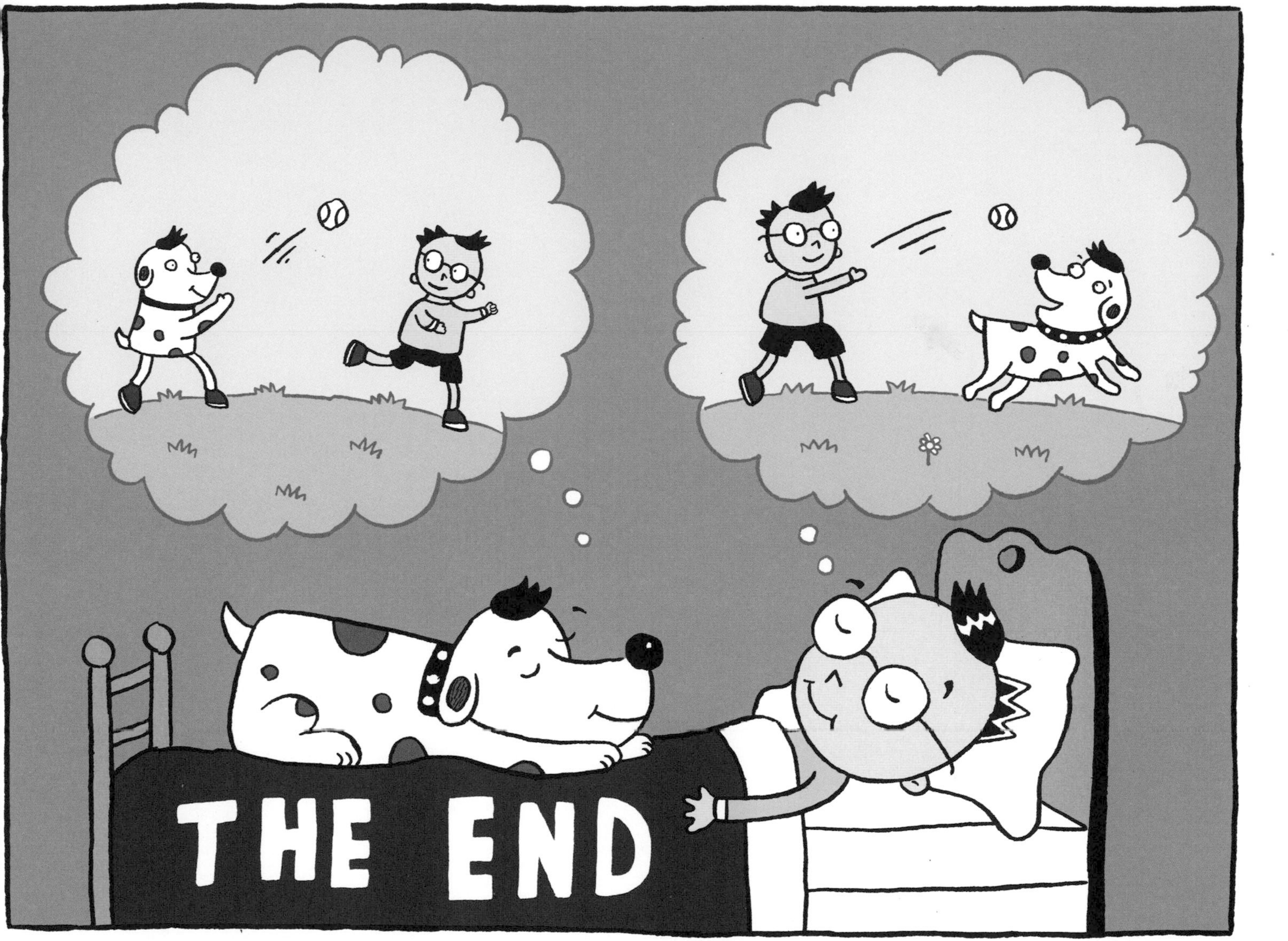
THE END

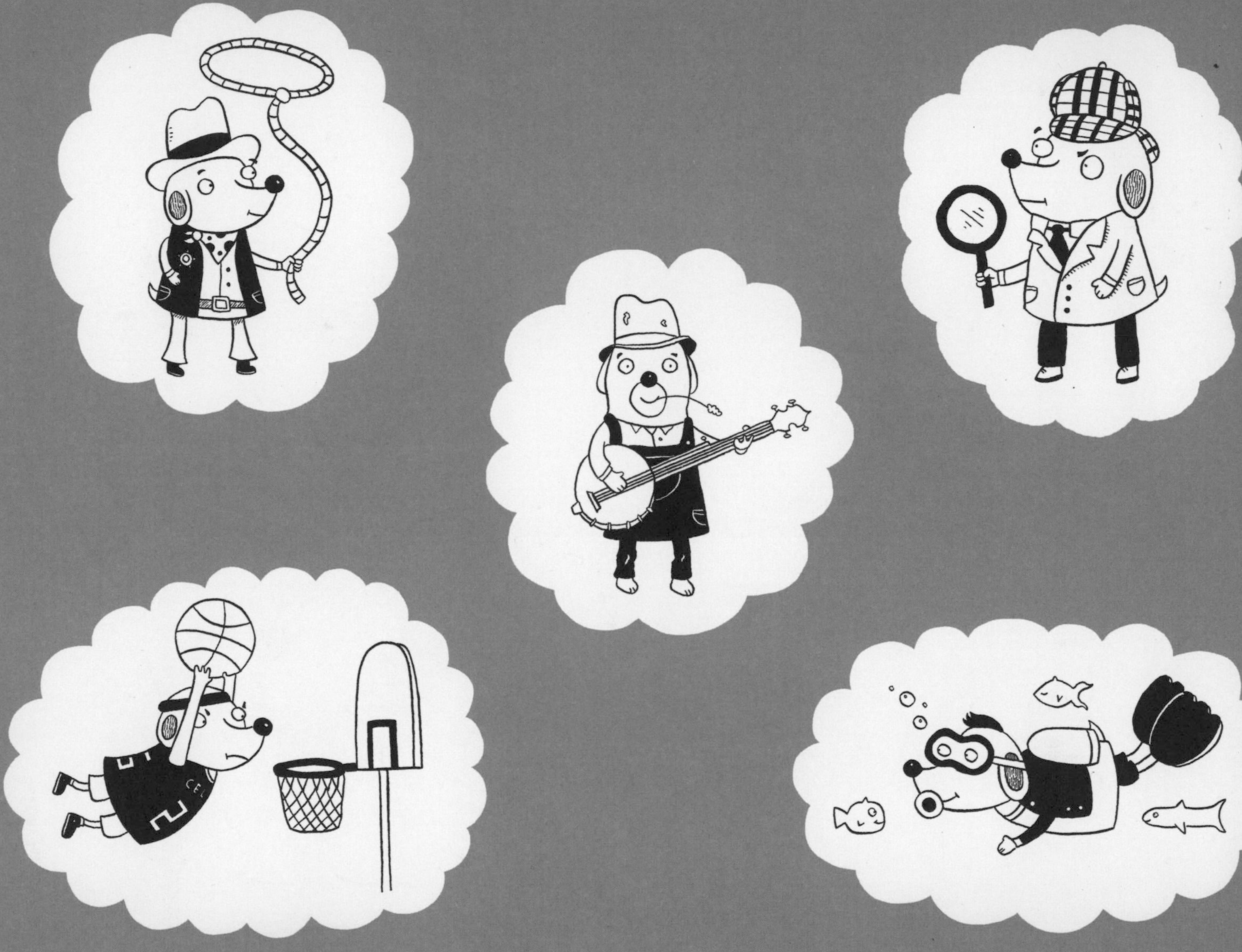